I0564267

The Weight of Sin

A novel

By
Simon Vincent
Author of Waypoint 90 and Sea Lust

www.simonvincent.com

Also by Simon Vincent

Fiction
Waypoint 90

Poetry
Sea Lust

Book and Cover design by Frank L. Fernandez.
Type Set is Book Antigua.

First Edition

Author Notes

This is a fictional story set in present time, any similarities real or implied between my characters and any living person is pure coincidence. Not one of my characters is drawn from a living or deceased person. However some of the individuals, organizations, and events portrayed in this book are based on historical fact, such as the assault on the Japanese Ambassadors residence in Lima, Peru and the organizations known as the Sendero Luminoso (Shining Path) and Movimiento Revolucioniario Tupac Amaru (MRTA). Below are detailed footnotes on these Individuals and Organizations. I present them to the reader to enhance their reading experience.

The Shining Path "Sendero Luminoso" had manifested itself into the consciousness of the Peruvian people. It attracted the communists and neo-communists as well as the students and liberals with a popular stand against the ruling elite. The ones in charge were the enemy of the people; it did not matter who they were. They fueled hatred among the classes and specifically fomented long forgotten resentment among the Inca people, the once mighty Incas of the highlands where the girl's mother came from.

But the "Path" was still reeling from the capture and imprisonment of their charismatic Maoist leader Abimael

Guzman in 1992. Their new leadership lacked the guidance that Guzman had provided. Their impact was relegated to the highlands and their acts of terrorism seemed impotent against the ruling class.

MRTA-Tupac Amaru Revolutionary Movement (Spanish: Movimiento Revolucioniario Tupac Amaru, abbreviated MRTA) A Marxist urban guerrila group that took its name from Tupac Amaru II (1780-c. 1782) the last indigenous leader of the Incas who led a valiant but failed insurrection of his people along with the mestizo peasants against the Spaniards in the 18th century. At the height of its power they had several hundred active members committed to Socialist ideologies with the purpose to replace the ruling elite and replace it with homegrown leaders eliminating all imperialist elements from society. The group was active during the 1980's up to 1997 fomenting instability and fear in the country, its influence was severely diminished in 1997 when its leaders were killed or sent to prison.

Fidel Castro (1926-) is Cuba's homegrown dictator. The illegitimate son of a successful Creole sugar plantation owner was born in Cuba in 1926. He is the sad answer to so much corruption and political instability in an island nation spoiled by its close proximity to the United States enjoying all the benefits of America's free enterprise system yet none of the constitutional stability. Castro changed all that. Showing so much promise and backed by popular demand   when he took over in 1959, he betrayed all who believed in him by becoming the worst dictator in the history of Latin America. He is the absolute leader of Cuba. What he says is law, his whims, his bungling handling of the economy and especially his explicit hatred of the United States was subsidized by the Soviet Bloc until the fall of Communism. Many thought he was finished when the Soviet Union collapsed. But Fidel just kept on feeding his followers new lies and creating in Cuba an eco-system very similar to Haiti, where there is small ruling elite and a huge starving mass of humanity. This is the reality of Cuba today as Fidel awaits death overcome with disease that finally has made him transfer authority to his brother Raul. The Cuban people hope that like all ruthless totalitarian regimes the end of this painful experiment is near.

Jose Marti (1853-1895) is the heart soul of the Cuban people. Recognized as a national hero by all Cubans even by Fidel Castro, he is the true revolutionary patriot. His was the passionate voice of the Cuban revolution against Spain at the turn of the century. A poet and prolific writer of pamphlets extolling his people to revolt against the Spanish, he traveled the world uniting all to his one goal in life: a free Cuba. He was born of Spanish parents and studied in Spain but nonetheless he was one of the central figures along with Antonio Maceo in the struggle for independence. He never lived to see Cuba free. And if he could see the current   leader Fidel Castro he would be turning over in his grave with the realization of the current state of the Cuba that he championed.

Antonio Maceo (Lt. General José Antonio de la Caridad Maceo y Grajales (1845-1896) was second-in-command of the Cuban Army of Independence. He was born of Venezuelan parents in Cuba. If Jose Marti was its heart and soul Maceo was the sword, the man of action, the George Washington of Cuba. Revered by his followers and troops he was known as "The Bronze Titan", which was a reference to his skin color. Also known as the "Greater Lion". Maceo was Cuba's most successful military strategists and guerrilla leaders. His military feats became the stuff of legends. His tactics of guerrilla and open warfare inflicted a cost on the Spanish Army of more than a quarter million soldiers. He overcame Spanish blockades and traps and traveled the entire island of Cuba usually having to deal with overwhelming technical and numerical odds. His coordination of chain of command in the revolutionary war made him invaluable in the struggle for Independence. Like Marti he would never see his beloved Cuba Free. He was killed in an insignificant skirmish towards the end of the struggle alongside one of his Luitenents, Francisco "Panchito" Gómez Toro who legend says tried to protect him. The remains of Antonio Maceo and his loyal Luitenent "Panchito" lie in a monument in Cuba and the site is one of pilgrimage by Cuban people.

Hiram Bingham III- (1875-1956). The explorer that is credited with re-discovering the "Lost City of the Incas", Machu Picchu in 1911. His bestselling book of the same title was a hit with readers in 1948. Many historians and Present day moviegoers consider him a role model for the "Indiana Jones" character. Bingham was a colorful adventurer and treasure hunter who listened to and was guided by local Inca farmers who led him to the ruins. Machu Picchu is today one of the major tourist attractions in South America. Bingham among others helped bring the incredible ruins to the worldwide public. The zig zag road from Aguas Calientes that brings the tour buses and brave drivers to the site is named the Hiram Bingham Highway. He later served as a US senator.

Alberto Ken'ya Fujimori-Born July 28 1938-President of Peru from his 52nd Birthday, July 28, 1990 to November 17, 2000. He was a controversial figure from the day he entered politics to the present day as he serves out his prison sentence.

Fujimori rose to the heights of popularity when he fought against terrorism in Peru and restored economic and political stability. He used every method he could to achieve his goals, authoritarianism, human rights violations, and more. However misguided, his actions brought about the downfall of "The Shining Path" and the "MRTA" terrorist groups.

A Peruvian of Japanese descent, he fled to Japan in 2000, he was in the midst of his self-imposed exile when he visited Chile in November 2005 he was arrested and finally extradited to face criminal charges of corruption and human rights abuses. In 2008 when he was convicted the majority of Peruvians polled, voiced approval for his leadership during this difficult and bloody period.

Simon Vincent
Miami, Florida

For
Ariana, Vince, and Frank

"It is not the works, but the *belief* which is here decisive and determines the order of rank--to employ once more an old religious formula with a new deeper meaning,--it is some fundamental certainty which a noble soul has about itself, something which is not to be sought, is not to be found, and perhaps, also, is not to be lost.- *The noble soul has reverence for itself."*

(Friedrich Nietzsche, *Beyond Good and Evil.*)

Prologue

Havana, Cuba July 13, 1989

Colon Cemetery Havana

The burial was complete. A heavy set soldier wearing a dirty and sweaty undershirt under his army BDU's (fatigues) was placing the final pieces of sod on the fresh soil. His name was David, he was half Jewish. He was born a Jew but raised by his Catholic mother who had converted to Judaism to please his father before they married, she raised her son alone after his father left them behind during the Mariel exodus and went to the

14

United States with a promise   to send for them, they stopped
waiting when they found out he had married a wealthy Jewish
heiress in New York City.

He had a sad look about him. His almost bald head
glistened with sweat, as he worked the last square piece of
Bermuda grass into place and backed away reverently. He never
changed expression the whole time he was there. He did not
want to be there.

He had been picked for an assignment in the "Special
Troops" Military base in Playa Baracoa, a beach town in West
Havana, at the last minute he was diverted and ordered to climb
into the rear of a covered army truck that had a canvas door
covering the back cabin. Once he climbed in he sat on an empty
bench next to the only other thing inside; a sealed wooden coffin.

David Lester Gurinsky was a lot smarter than the
impression he gave to his fellow soldiers and officers. He knew
that the body in the coffin was important. He wished he hadn't
followed the trials that ended with the death sentences and he
wished he didn't speculate about who was in the coffin. But he
had a damn good idea. The drive from the seashore to the inner
city was quiet, it was still early and the morning traffic was very
light.

He had too much time to think and speculate about the
next few hours. He went to the canvas cover and peeked out. A
green Mercedes was following the truck as well as two
unmarked cars that he figured were secret police. His stomach
churned up the espresso he had enjoyed so much just minutes

before.

He sat back and tried not to think.

When he saw the men that met the truck at Colon cemetery, his fears exacerbated and he felt the familiar tingling in his chest and down his arms forewarning an anxiety attack. It almost arrived with the order to get out of the truck. He recognized one of them immediately and for a moment he thought about trying to run away or faking illness. Now he knew for sure who was in the coffin. But he began to pray to himself, silent Hail Mary's and played the usual dumb soldier.

Now just minutes later that seemed like hours, David stood alongside the four men as they stared at the patch of fresh grass. He peeked cautiously from one man to the other, studying them.

General Raul Leonardo Marban, head of the Eastern Army of the Cuban Armed Forces was the highest ranking of the four, followed by Gen. Victor Luis Salgado, Chief of the Military's Special Troops who had put a final bullet into the head of the dead general lying in the coffin six feet below their feet. The oldest of the group was Soviet General Vassili Petrov who wept in stoic silence, he was a legend to the Cuban troops, and he could see the tears make their way slowly down the ruddy face of the old man who had won the hearts and souls of the rank and file while fighting with them in the African campaigns. The last man, the youngest, he did not recognize, but he knew he was a medical officer from his uniform insignia.

David knew right then and there that the man that lay buried beneath him was innocent. The charges of treason were trumped up by a failing regime and by a weakening leader who feared men of courage who had won the loyalty of the Army by fighting and bleeding alongside them in the fields of battle. These men who stood by and watched and let him be executed were more afraid than him. The faintest grin began to form on his face. Even the mighty fear something greater than themselves. It gave him comfort. He prayed for the man he buried by asking God to forgive his trespasses and accept him into heaven. He stood there feeling proud, full of vigor and he knew he would be all right. He buried the shovel in the ground, slipped on his army shirt and leisurely walked away.

The four men never looked away from the grave, after awhile they each saluted the grave and their friend in silence one last time.

Alexander

"You have your brush, you have your colors, you paint paradise, then in you go."

Nikos Kazantzakis, author

1

*"Oh how we stretch our
lifelines when we clutch
the weight of sin!"*

--Jose Manuel Garcia

Miami, Florida 1993

A slow-moving tear snaked down Alex's cheek as he looked aimlessly out of his bedroom balcony for one last time. One tear, perhaps out of regret or pity or humanity. Outside, the pre-dawn blackness enveloped the neighboring buildings in the plush Brickell Avenue neighborhood of Miami. He looked out at the expansive view of Biscayne Bay and farther on to the distant lights on the shoreline of Key Biscayne. The fresh smell of the approaching dawn was strong. Hardly anything stirred. A soothing, reassuring calmness   cuddled him like a warm blanket on a cold night. He took it all in for a few breathtaking moments. Then painfully, the first few sounds of life pierced him and he felt that familiar dull numbing pain in the middle of his forehead. It was time.

He was frozen in place for a few seconds, breathing slowly, rhythmically. He opened his eyes, dark like the night, intensely set in a handsome face. The whites of his eyes were red and sore, not used to tears and lack of sleep. He is almost thirty years old, but feels twice that today. His hair is dark brown with one or two fairly new gray strands around the temples. The hair is longish and growing naturally without a definite style or cut.

His skin is white, with a trace of a natural tan. But he is taller than most Latinos, just over six feet with broad, thick shoulders carrying a bit more weight than when he played minor league baseball. God! How the old man loved to see him pitch and hit, and just play ball. Just underneath and to the right of his neck there is a scar where they fixed his clavicle from the motorcycle crash that ended his promising career. He could have pitched again, but he took the accident as an omen and gave up the game. It broke his father's heart. They cried together at that time. Now he realized that his father had wanted it more than him. He was through living someone else's dream. His father had written him a long letter as an apology for his behavior at the end of his playing career. He ended by writing:

"And together we are…poet warriors,
Journeymen of the sea, keepers of the truth in love!
My Son, I love you!"

The words were hollow.

He was focused now. Destiny beckoned.

He suddenly realizes that he is naked. He runs his hands over the hairs on his chest and trails the hair down his stomach to his manhood.

The quiet hypnotic moment is broken suddenly by a squawking seagull that flies past him on the balcony. It does not faze him. He grins. The new force is there, he feels its power.

But now he is aware of the clamor of the "early-birds" driving sixteen floors below on Brickell Avenue in the dark so anxious to get to their Downtown offices ahead of their co-workers, some were genuine workaholics some just wanted to impress.

At last he shuts his eyes for a few seconds. Tears want to flow but he fights them back into that dark place where they have been festering far too long. He turns to face the room.

Through the open sliding glass doors the sheer curtains are billowing softly in the breeze. The thin cloth is the only thing stirring as he looks inside. The bedroom…her bedroom, with the handpicked modern expensive Scandinavian furniture, to the Brazilian carpet and finally to the Botero and Monet's Lillies on the wall. Expensive reproductions that they bought in Paris, when his life was full of hope and love.   He looks past his favorite spot. The big overstuffed chair spilling over with discarded clothing. He walks over and slips on custom tailored slacks. Very fine Italian styling with a perfect crease that runs down and will barely brush the imported leather of his Ferragamos.

As he sits on the overburdened chair tying his shoelaces he turns and looks at the bed with his new eyes. On the bed with the covers half discarded lays the beautiful naked body of his wife, her body askew on the bed from one corner to the other, she always slept like that taking charge of their bed, unlike his efficient way of taking just enough space on one side to lie sideways, and mostly away from her these last few weeks. She is a young blond haired woman with milky white skin. She sleeps peacefully hardly stirring. She is truly divine.

He looks at her for a moment, devoid of expression. He can control himself for a few more minutes.

He makes his way to the dresser and places the letter on top of the polished mahogany surface.

He slips on a linen shirt the color of charcoal and grabs the two designer leather bags sitting by the door.

It is not until he is driving on the overseas highway passing Islamorada in the Florida Keys that he begins to feel the release that comes with acceptance of the angst-ridden events that torment him.

2

Miami, Florida three months later.

The smell of jasmine always reminded him of the house in Coconut Grove.

He drank from a small styrofoam cup, the last few drops of the espresso making him almost human.

The dawn of the new day was fast approaching.

> *Come, Aurora, share with us*
> *The light and the morning's dew*
> *On your velvet cloak that brightly brings*
> *The promise of hope anew this day.*

They are just words now, but they haunt him still.

He stood on the sidewalk in front of the small wood frame home inhaling the salt in the breeze that comes from the bay waters of Dinner Key, just two blocks away. But it is the scent of the night-blooming jasmine that brings him back. It permeates his nostrils and hangs suspended in mid-air like a copious fog.

The branches are bigger now. The Jasmine has grown along the side of the porch that shapes the entire front of the house. It is a fairly large porch that in the time he lived here had wooden slatted shutters that are not used anymore, not efficient at keeping the cool air-conditioned atmosphere of the modern homes. It was precisely for just that reason that his mother and father had chosen the home. It was airy, comfortable, and the closest they could afford to live near the sea they loved.

The house is on Aviation Avenue just after the turn from the busy intersection of Bird Road and 27th Ave. The Grove location was bittersweet. The nearby intersection was well known to offer all the marijuana and sex a young man could afford. His mother looked the other way. His father lectured him about the evil weed and exotic diseases. He still sampled all the goodies and felt all the guilt and remorse of a boy growing up his own man.

It was a house of happy memories until that fateful day.

Over on the steps he had carried his beloved cousin Donna when he was just a teenager, showing off the strength of a boy-not-quite-a-man. His mother took a photo that was proudly displayed next to the one of Donna carrying him when he was just a baby and she a young girl of twelve   enthralled by her new male cousin. How he loved his cousin, the stolen kisses and caresses in the back yard behind the garage, hidden from the world in the shadows of the mango and avocado trees. She was gone, now only a memory. Cancer took her swiftly just a few years before his parent's death. Tears always followed a thought of her, but not today, perhaps not ever again.

He used to park his metallic green 1965 Mustang Fastback with the 289HP engine and four-on-the-floor in the carport at the end of the driveway towards the rear of the house. Under the carport his buddies would meet and play dominoes for hours after swimming in the bay and diving off the Fair Isle Bridge on those long hot summer days. For years Fair Isle was just an empty piece of coral sand, pine trees and mangroves. But someone had built a bridge in the hopes of developing the beautiful location; it would be twenty years before the entire island would be devoured by high priced condos. His mother fed them hotdogs and ham and cheese sandwiches, and marveled at how many they could consume at one sitting. Especially "Lagarto", "the lizard", the one with the big nose and the stutter, he was the best. And as ironic fate would have it, he was the thinnest of all. He could eat them all under the table. He could see them all munching away as they made fun of "Lagarto".

He walked along the side of the house and stood in the carport next to the gold Mercedes SUV parked underneath, looking at the backyard and the detached garage at the rear in the northwest corner of the yard. He wondered if the magazines would still be there behind the loose wall panel near the small bathroom where he would masturbate in seclusion. During the heat of summer he would emerge from the small toilet soaked in sweat. He shook his head at the memory. He walked back up to the front of the house and now stood almost on the entry steps leading up to the porch.

Near the corner of the porch facing the bay there is a huge window. His mother had hung plants just right so that an air of nature was inside the house. The plants, some sitting on pots in the windowsill and some hanging with flowers of various colors along with philodendrons, framed the window. It was a peaceful bright spot made for reading and writing. If you strained your sight far enough you could just catch a glimpse of the water on Biscayne Bay and the tops of the masts of the sailboats moored in Mutiny bay. His father would sit by that window for hours reading his newspapers, magazines and the endless books. His mother would do the same when his father was not home. He smiled again and remembered that he would also use the old overstuffed chair when neither of them was around to read his comic books and the many books that his father suggested to him along with the ones he chose for himself. His father's choices were always harder to read and understand but now he was glad he read them, each with a special bond to the old man. Especially *The Old Man and The Sea*. He remembered the time when he was just beginning to read adult books when his father sat with him and read the short novel to him

in English so that he could understand it better. During stressful
episodes in his life he would pick up the same well-worn copy and
read it in one sitting, somehow expecting the great marlin to make
it to shore just one time, it soothed him to read it, it was his
sedative. It had not worked just a few weeks ago. He had ripped
the book to shreds and thrown the scraps like confetti from his
balcony.

It was a good spot.

The assassin had stood behind the jasmine bush just outside
that window and fired the bullet through the glass into his father's
head just above the right ear, forever sealing Alex's fate.

> *"My blood flows. Broken shards of glass surround
> me. Fragments of my life, every piece a secret. No one to
> hold me, this time. Through the pretty picture...a human
> bullet...no! A cannonball! No one to offer a helping hand.
> All alone but alive except for the blood of my soul. And
> my eyes so wide--no time for a blink or a sigh--but
> everything was so nice."*

His mother's last words written in mindless stupor and left
for him just a few months later, before she cut her wrists with a
shard of glass from the broken window, just words now, but they
still haunted him. He had lacked her courage then; but now was
the time.

He drank the last of his espresso and with a flick from his

Gold Calibri lighter lit his last   cigarette. He had made many changes the last few weeks. Giving up smoking would be easy. Getting in shape was slower, and shedding the excess weight had been difficult. But there is a new resolve in his thinking. A new attitude. A new current is sucking him out to uncharted seas.

He had spent these last few weeks living aboard a 33 foot Hunter sailboat that he had rented in Marathon. He sailed almost every day, sometimes staying out for days living on the fish he caught along with fruit and vegetables that when combined with the rigors of sailing helped him shape his new physique. He took this time to think to meditate and to shape his future.

It was the end of innocence... of happy dreams and fantasies of love and fame. Gone were the days of wasted opportunities and wallowing in self-pity. There will be no more reminiscing and revisiting those warm soft memories about a loving family, a public father's patriotism and a mother's soothing touch.

He surrendered to loss. He languished not in despair but indifference, and release and then renewal. The burnout and sadness his friends perceived was in fact his transfiguration. Like the Phoenix, born again from the flames, he was a new creature.

He had thought it all out for the very first time in his life. The cathartic realization that his life ended the same day his father was killed was painful at first and then powerful. For so long he had no idea of where he was going. He had lost his foundation; his faith followed taking his soul. His values and structure became obscured. But now he knew.

There are no slatted shutters anymore; they were replaced by square smoke glass windows that open to the side and are very efficient at keeping the cool air inside. Inside the house the lights came on. He stood in the middle of the walkway, a few feet from the front steps. He felt the calm of the darkness around him; comfortably cloaked in its blackness. His fingertips tingled. He is aroused by totally new stimuli. It is not unpleasant. A cat scurries from under the bushes and runs across the street.

The front door slowly opened. A man appeared behind a safety chain, a woman huddled beside him. They were half dressed, a middle-aged couple who enjoyed their nice home.

Would they recognize him? He gambles they would not.

"What do you want?" The man's voice was controlled, but frightened. He is almost bald now and over 60 pounds overweight. He was a powerful attorney with political ties at one time. A man of influence. That was before he began to work for Alex's father.

How he had taken control of the assets of his father's foundation took him by surprise. He remembered only the legal documents that he read incredulously telling him he had no rights to the property unless he came up with a payment of $100,000. He did not have the money or the inclination to get it. While still mourning he let it lapse and his option expired. When he called the attorney who he now faced, he was told it was business. He was sorry but everything was legal and he had bought the house from the Estate.

There was a malevolent confidence befitting his newfound

force as he stood just feet from   the two faces and looked into their eyes. They did not recognize the man-demon before them.

They both saw it then. *The eyes.* Their faces contort, the woman ran back into the interior of the house.

"We...called the police..." It comes out like a piteous plea, a whimper, that precise moment when the prey feels the jaws of the predator around his neck.

The attorney shut the door and ran into their home.

Alex stood a few seconds more enjoying the last draw from his last cigarette; savoring the hunt.

He flicked the butt at the house and strode to the door. A powerful kick and the door caved in. He walked to the man and the woman as they fervently tried to speak on the telephone drawing a pistol from his belt. He yanked the receiver from the man's hand and threw him against the wall shoving the black Glock pistol into his throat. The woman screamed and he slapped her forcefully with the back of his free hand. She whirled falling with a heavy thud on the dining table. He hit the man with the butt of his gun and he slumped into a heap on the polished hardwood floor.

He goes to the woman frozen with fear and begging for mercy. He takes a hand towel that was resting on the table wraps it around her mouth and ties it around the back of her head and shoved her face down on the kitchen table. The flimsy house dress tears easily; she is naked under her dress. Her body is flabby and shows the signs of age and avarice. He does not care; her body is not what he is after... it's her soul. He reached for the bottle of olive oil in a decorative crystal   decanter and poured a stream of liquid in between the cheeks of her buttocks. The woman whimpers through the fabric, she reaches up and frees her mouth.

"Please, please don't hurt me…"

He hesitated for a fraction of a moment then shoved her roughly from the table and she fell heavily on the floor sobbing.

"You make me sick, you fat piece of shit!"

The lawyer opened his eyes. A whimpering sound came from his mouth as he sees his wife naked on their expensive parquet floor gripped with fear and sobbing hysterically.

Alex goes to the man and places the barrel of the Glock in his mouth. Tears roll down his cheeks as he tries to speak choking on his saliva. He hesitated again. He looked inside the human eyes of his prey, total submission. He grins.

"BANG!" He whispered roughly. Then he hit him again with the barrel of the gun across his mouth hurling several teeth through the air before the bald head hits the floor.

Alex was disgusted. Nausea let him know he was still human.

He moved away quietly facing the wretched pair.

The helpless couple would not report the assault, just the break-in; vanity would shield him from the violence of his vengeance. He then quickly walked out of the house and slipped away into the half-light.

Illapa

"Like cars in amusement parks, our direction is often determined through collisions."

-*Yahia Lababidi, author*

3

The Highlands of Peru, near Machu Picchu 1994

The girl Illapa chewed the coca leaves slowly. The pungent raw flavor of the mystical leaves reminding her of the little girl of not so long ago. She had not thought about that girl for a long time. But now there was no time for thinking or for growing up, it was a time for staying alive.   She carried a 9mm Beretta; a present from one of her mother's many boyfriends that she traded for her virginity when she turned fourteen almost four years ago. Soon she would get an automatic rifle, an AK 47 or an American M16; yes she would love an American assault weapon. In her mind they were the best.

Her mother had told her that everything that was best was in America, the Land of Opportunity. She should go there someday. Find her pot of gold. Marry a gringo and live the good life.

For now she was happy to belong to the group and carry a gun, fight for freedom and equality, and take the country back from the filthy corrupt pigs that stole it from the people.

The girl had long straight raven black hair. Like black silk it had a natural shine. The kind of shine most women pay top dollar for designer products to achieve. It had grown down to her waist. But she kept it bundled under her canvas cap. She would only let it loose when she bathed. She did not even let it loose when she had sex. She didn't want her hair contaminated with a manly musk. It was defiance. It was independence.

Her face was oval with high cheekbones. It was a European face to match her emerald green eyes. Her skin was her mother's dark complexion but several shades lighter. Her breasts were the size of small mangoes, just perfect to go without a bra and more than enough to make men look with lust. Her body was naturally lean. She was a good head taller than most of the Inka women. She stood out in a crowd for her height and her beauty. However she dressed like the men, military style boots and green fatigues that she borrowed permanently from the men in her group. She blended better with the men than the women. It was all business with her.

The "Sendero Luminoso" The Shinning Path had manifested itself into the consciousness of the Peruvian people. It attracted the communists and neo-communists as well as the students and liberals with a popular stand against the ruling elite. The ones in charge were the enemy of the people; it did not matter who they were. They fueled hatred among the classes and specifically fomented long forgotten resentment among the Inka people, the once mighty Incas of the highlands where the girl's mother came from.

But the "Path" was still reeling from the capture and imprisonment of their charismatic Maoist leader Abimael Guzman in 1992. Their new leadership lacked the guidance that Guzman had provided. Their impact was relegated to the highlands and their acts of terrorism seemed impotent against the ruling class.

She had learned the truth about her birth from a letter her father wrote to her a few years earlier.

> *My dear daughter:*
>
> *Please forgive me. I should not have abandoned you and your mother. I wish I could have my life to do over, I would have acted differently. I write this in the hope that you read it someday and forgive me for I think of you and your mother often. I want to tell you our story so that you can know who you are.*
>
> *As you know your mother was K'uychi, which means Rainbow. She was a beautiful dark-skinned raven-haired descendant of the ancient Incas, and the daughter of a local chieftain, Kusi Tupaq, one of those few clinging to the land and the past.*
>
> *I am your Father. An army Colonel, my name is Pedro Sarmiento Lescault. I abducted K'uychi as*

she bathed in a stream. I had not intended on taking her. My orders were very strict not to add fuel to the fire already ignited by the guerrillas. But something provoked me as I saw her naked beauty in that stream. Like Aecton from mythology watching Diana, I was powerless. I was mesmerized and acted on impulse. Only I was not turned into a stag like poor Aecton. The reality of my destiny would exact a different but just as cruel a fate for me.

After abducting her I did not violate her nor allow my men to even come near her. Instead I became her servant, her slave. I romanced her in this bizarre and passive way and slowly and tenderly she gave herself to me. We fell in love. She melted in my arms as we made love. Our skin color so starkly different. My white skin and light eyes enthralled your mother. She loved my green eyes, "pale as the landscape" she would say. The only thing she hated was the blemish on my skin caused by a tattoo of the family crest featuring a fleur de lis on my arm.

We lived in the highlands between Qosqo (Cuzco) and Machu Picchu, where I had been stationed and where I had established a frontier outpost endorsed by the Peruvian Army. My duties were clear: break the guerrillas' ties with the peasants. I decided after much soul-searching that taking a local for a   bride would help me fit in. And alas it did. We went back to your grandfather, even though he was prepared to kill me, and I persuaded Kusi Tupac to allow me to take K'uychi for my bride, with his reluctant blessing. Some of my men followed suit and for a while all seemed bliss. I was praised as an innovator and benefactor. The guerrillas avoided our territory and the brass in Lima took great pleasure in extolling my virtues and creating a mythical figure popular with all the classes.

But in the end politics would interfere. Peru's ruling elite would change and I was called to Lima to face a tribunal. It was a time of political turmoil and I lost all my previous support and allegiances.

It ended badly. I was ordered to stay in Lima and my replacement forcibly returned the Incas to their homes and forbade any more intimate contact with them under the penalty of court order or death.

Your mother K'uychi arrived at your grandfathers' village where I was told she gave birth to a beautiful girl who they named Illapa.

My lovely Illapa, I long for your touch, your presence and love. I have prayed for you and your mother but all my prayers have proven fruitless and I grow discouraged and in despair. I hope to

someday find you and give you and your
mother a better life. For now I send you a father's
love.

Your Father,
Pedro Sarmiento Lescault

Pedro Sarmiento Lescault was not born a soldier. His lifelong ambition was to be a man of God. He wanted to be a priest. When he was a boy of twelve he visited the museum of El Prado in Madrid Spain with his family, and standing below a painting of El Greco depicting the crucifixion of Christ, he felt a calling. That night sitting at the dinner table he came right out and told his family. "I want to become a priest and then a monk and study here in Spain in a Monastery and then go home and serve my people."

His mother was startled but not shocked, she knew that there was greatness in her son, but she never imagined the Church. His father was in total disbelief. A landowner and member of the House of Representatives, all he wanted from his son was that he study the law and follow in his footsteps, perhaps a run at the presidency in his future.

"Are you totally out of your mind!" his father admonished.

"Papa, all I want is to serve God and help my fellow man."

He stood his ground. Later that night his mother came

into his room.

"My precious son, I'm so proud of you this day. I could not be happier to see you become a man of God, but give me some time to talk to your father. Come here, do you know how special you are to me."

She held him close like mothers often do and brushed his hair.

"You can do anything you set your heart to do, you are so much more serious and mature than all your friends, and you stand head and shoulders above them all."

She placed him on a pedestal and he could see for the first time in his life his future. He saw himself kneeling in prayer in a gilded chapel at the foot of the cross.

But his father would not budge. As soon as they returned he made the arrangements and sent him to a Military boarding school. Asking him to graduate from High School before deciding on a career. He assured his father that it would not make a difference, he would become a monk.

In the end his father was right. By the end of his senior year he had risen to his mother's pedestal, and had become the head of his class and the head of the Corp of cadets. From which the army came calling and all but guaranteed his rise to the top by having him choose his commission, he chose the rural militia. He wanted to do right by the Incas, whose land they shared and whose race was in decline. He would do what he could to make it right.

4

The jungle march was going well. For two days and nights they made their way through the Warmiwanuska Pass, Illapa had traveled this road several times with her grandfather going through the slow descents and dense paths through the thin air. The coca leaves helped. And she saw the discomfort of the ones in the group that were not used to the terrain.

Her mother had told her many stories about the coca leaves and their close ties to the Incan people. The Incans considered the leaves magical and powerful. Her grandfather was an elder and controlled the special leaves and their use and distribution for a large portion of the area, he was powerful on his own but the coca leaves gave him more control over his people, but he never exploited them, he balanced their role as an important commodity and for religious rituals.

She was glad for the group when they stopped near a stream within sight of the small valley she recognized as Pakaymayu (the hidden river).

The girl chewed her leaves and helped others by showing them how to chew them and hold their liquid in their mouths before swallowing.

When the march resumed the spirits of the most tired were lifted by the girls tutoring.

Like her grandfather had taught her the group avoided the thick vegetation and kept to ancient trails that meander in perfect harmony with the mountainside. She had already guessed at their destination, the Aobamba Valley, and she knew that it was just a short hike ahead.

They arrived to a small clearing that her grandfather used as a base camp and she remembered sleeping under the stars for several days with him not long before. The spot was surrounded by a barrier of trees, her grandfather had told her about all of them intimpa, romerillo and uncas, with their roots and bases covered by several species of lichens, mosses and ferns, she could not remember all their names. But when she saw a cluster of Wakanki she marveled at its beauty, the flower was her favorite as well as her grandfathers the name meaning "You'll cry".

She had not cried in a very long time and wondered if she would ever again.

Javier, her squad leader and also her mentor and current lover, came to her group. He was a tall handsome aristocrat from Arequipa who brought money to join the cause. His tousled hair and boyish beard exposed him for the immature child in a man's body that he was. But he was stately, and his stern demeanor inspired loyalty in some of the peasants. He was ten years her senior.

"We are here; you have your orders and know the plan, now go and fight for the people!" Javier extolled them.

They acknowledged him each in their way, a wink, a nod, a look.

The girl stood apart from the others and admired several different wild orchids, each more colorful than the next. She reached out with her small delicate hand to feel their tender petals, remembering how her grandfather had adorned his house with some very similar to these.

Javier came to her and led her away to speak in private.

"How is my girl?" He asked, trying for tenderness but coming out condescending and shallow.

The girl did not respond. She did not much care for his words. They were empty and meaningless. She took from him what she wanted and played her part when he wanted a girl. She could be his girl, or she could be a cold-blooded killer. Right now she wanted nothing more than to get on with the show. She cocked her Beretta and looked   straight into his eyes.

"Let's go!"

And then Javier saw it for the first time.

The eyes!

He felt the cold chill down his spine. The fear of the prey.

She grabbed him around his neck and brought his face to hers, kissing his lips forcefully. It was like a transfer. She took his manhood and forced courage into him.

The column had begun to move quickly. She left him standing and joined the others.

They came to the secluded house at the end of the winding dirt road. It stood in semi-darkness in the cool moonlit country night. One had to know where to find it. But for a man searching for that special release no journey is too long or difficult. Mireya's whorehouse was the best of the region, well known for the young girls, poor peasants "sold" by their family for the quick dollar. The younger, the better. Ten to twelve was not rare.

The girl and her group were positioned to one side of the house. From her vantage point she could see the officers' bodyguards smoking and talking loudly in the front of the house, next to their military jeeps. There were four, heavily armed with automatic weapons. Maybe one of those would soon be hers.

Two young men came down the road singing and carrying bottles of pisco. Arm in arm they made their way to the soldiers. The men thought nothing of the ordinary looking pair of drunks.

Just before the soldiers could let them know that the house was closed until the military were finished, the young revelers pulled pistols from under their　　shirts and pumped a barrage of

bullets into the first two guards. As the other two prepared to fire, a barrage of automatic fire cut them down from the woods to their right. The younger of the two pretend drunkards, the one carrying the bottles, was hit in the leg by the crossfire and went down.

The main assault on the house came from the rear, where a planted guerrilla, one of the youngest girls, had opened the door and let the attackers into the house.

Illapa's group was to stay behind and cover the left flank and the entrance. She could smell the gunpowder and hear the loud retorts of the shots coming from the house amidst the cries of hysteria and agony.

Without warning, she sprung from the woods alone and attacked the front entrance. She ran low to the ground like a well-trained soldier, only no one had taught her.

At the door she fired into the doorhandle and kicked it open. A flurry of bullets crashed around her, hitting the wooden door and its frame. A few of the flying splinters struck her in the face and neck. No pain, just sparks from the fire. She sprung into the house crouching low. In the corner a soldier turned to fire but his bulky rifle bumped into a piece of furniture. She aimed her gun and fired rapidly, both hands on the grip as Julian had taught her. She fired several rounds into the silhouette of the soldier, like the target cut-out in the practice range. He went down with a cry of anguish. On the other side of the room another soldier frozen with panic tried to aim his weapon. The girl walked over and shot him through his left eyesocket.

Inside the house the sound of sobbing women and girls mingled with the last rounds of fire. From the main hall of the house a guerrilla appeared and waved to her. He came forward and she recognized him as the second in command. A cigar butt tightly engrossed in the corner of his mouth with some of the tobacco juices tracing its way down to his chin and disappearing into his neck, he surveyed the room and went outside the house. When he came back he was accompanied by Julian and the rest of her group.

Julian looked around in utter amazement. His face was the color of the ashen floor of a peasant hut. He quietly went outside so they would not see him vomit.

The girl followed the officer into the house. They went room to room where the other guerrillas were searching for weapons and other valuable loot. In the last room they saw their leader leaning over a naked body of a man covered in blood. The leader, a short bookish man who resembled a teacher more than a guerrilla, came slowly to them and said it was the Colonel they had sought. He was beyond help.

The girl walked slowly to the body. She looked at the pale white skin beneath the blood. Then her eyes froze on the tattoo on the shoulder, the distinctive French "Fleur de lis". She felt no pity, just a dull ache in her heart. She reached up to the colonel's face and wiped the blood as best she could. She looked into his eyes; they were the same green, the same eyes she saw everyday in the mirror.

His lips moved to speak.

"Bless me, please, before I go...Forgive me father for I have sinned, but...I beg your mercy...take my soul..." he coughed blood and grimaced in pain. The girl soothed him until the coughing stopped and he tried to speak through the pain, but could not.

She traced a cross upon his forehead with her delicate fingers, and whispered "I forgive you; you may go to heaven and the peace of salvation". A smile began to form in the man's face. He closed his eyes.

She stood and fired a single bullet at the center of the cross.

The blast made everyone look at her. But they looked different. There was reverence. Respect.

"Niňa, what is your name?" The leader asked.

"Illapa" She said as she leaned close to the lifeless face and brushed her moist and warm lips to the cold-unfeeling smile of her father.

5

Kusi Tupacs Village, Peru May 1995

The woman who they now called Illapa the Princess, entered the village in glory and respect.

Her grandfather was ill and would not live out the year. She went to him first. He lived in the largest house near the center of the village where all the paths of the village led to it. Kusi Tupac spent his last days talking about God and became so absorbed in Christianity that his old friends abandoned him. But his granddaughter saw in him what the others did not see. She saw the same revered leader but through the eyes of a modern woman. She knew the old ways were gone forever. And so did he. They talked for a long time   without anyone present.

When she told him that there was no God he smiled at her gave her his Bible and said:

"My child, take this and read it. Perhaps not tonight, but someday. I am sure you will change your mind. You are like me, you love the past but know we must live in the present. Knowledge will bring you choices and one of these choices will be faith. You will find your faith as I have."

"You converted my mother… that was a miracle!"

"Have you seen her?"

"Not yet."

"You must forgive her!"

"I don't know if I can." She turned from him and looked around the house.

"She has suffered, and we are called to love and comfort her." He reached gently and held her hand in his.

"I have suffered too."

"Yes, and you will continue to suffer until your heart is ready. Then you will see what I saw with the eyes of my heart."

"I don't have time for God right now. I have to fight for my people with guns and bullets, not words and rosaries! I will fight for you, I am trying to make it right for what they have done to our people, how can you forgive their sins, and their God, where is he?"

"He is fighting with you, but one day you will see he fights with love and salvation. You will see!" He raised himself on his elbows to look her in   the eyes.

"My precious princess, you must let go of the hate. I did. You know that it was not very long ago that we were the greatest empire on this earth. We could have called ourselves the chosen people and I know many of my ancestors did. But the Spaniards vanquished us. I believe it was not only their modern ways but their God. When I think back all I feel is compassion for them and gratitude because they brought the real God to us. That same God they hid behind and committed those atrocities. But I shudder to think what would have happened if they did not bring their God with them. Perhaps the world would not exist. The men who came were sinners first and Christian second. That is the way I feel. They put their expansion, greed and lust before their God. But without God they would have been worse. There were many priests who came to us with those rosaries and bibles and showed us the way. Some of them perished alongside of us. Without God we would not have endured. In the end I know it was all God's plan for us." He turned away lowering himself back on the bed so that she would not see his weakened state. She sensed his discomfort.

"Grandfather, I will come back later, rest now." She kissed his forehead and walked away to the whisper of his voice.

"Vaya con Dios, mi niña."

Later that day.

The sun was fading over the hills. Soon the village would be enveloped in darkness. A dog barked somewhere in the shadows. Near the end of the village, in the east, a few men and women sat around a growing fire. On one side sat the village shaman, who looked and waved his staff at Illapa. Laughter was the first thing that crossed her mind as the group began to dance around the fire. They had been drinking pisco, a lot of pisco.

The Princess did not look at them, but continued her walk. When she came to the small house she paused and looked up at the sky and took a deep breath. She fought back the tears and kept them in their special dark place.

Once inside she faced her mother who was sitting in a rocking chair by the half-light of a kerosene lantern hanging above her head.

"Mi niňa, mi niña." She reached for her daughter.

"Mama."

The mother and daughter embrace and hold each other for a long time.

After a while the girl sits with her mother but after a few minutes the mother begins to cry. Her hands shake as she tries to hold a cup of hot tea. Illapa tries to hide her anger and pain from the woman who looks so much older than she remembers and who now sat in the chair with the stump of her leg showing under the hem of her dress.

How many years had it been? At least ten since she cared

how her mother responded,   since her responses had power over her. Then she had to wallow through another kind of similar muck with her father, but that too was now only a sad memory. So many times she thought she had been centered, had reached a balance. She rejoiced then in the strength she gained from her suffering. She reached an emotional plateau of sorts when she joined the struggle to relieve the suffering of her people. All those months spent with her comrades, her lovers, the nonviolent educational months of training and reading, clearing herself of the emotional baggage in order to make way for the responses of a heart dedicated to a just and noble cause.

She pleaded to her grandfathers' gods for the strength and guidance to succeed. To point her forward and allow her to regain her emotional stability so hard-won, so hard fought-for, so thoroughly gained. How would she deal with this new spiritual mother that had caused her so much pain?

"My lovely beautiful child, do you think it's easy to be a woman, to be loved, to love a man?" her mother spoke at long last. "I hated your father and myself for a long time, but I finally forgave him and myself and handed my life over to God. Now I only love; hate and anger are not in my life anymore."

"Well it's not going to be that easy for me. I hated him for so long. Now he's gone and I have no one to hate, so I hate them all! All those politicians and rich men who play with our lives like it was a game, they will pay for their kicks. Believe me they will pay!"

The old woman looked at her daughter moving about the

room like a caged jaguar, every now and then looking at her stump.

"I know about your anger and hate. I know about your pain. Those struggles and defeats are what made you who you are. But look at yourself deeply. Out of your pain a new woman has emerged. You are a strong vibrant descendant of our mighty ancestors. You must carry our history and make them hear you. But with God at your side."

"The same God who took your leg and made you a cripple?" she said sarcastically.

"Yes, the very same. He took my leg and almost killed me. And then He led me out of my hell and into his light." She pointed at her daughter with her walking stick.

"That day I was thrown from that car drugged out of my mind and run over several times on the main highway was the beginning of my new life. He took away my leg, and I pitied myself at the thought of losing my beauty and appeal. But He rescued me for my new life. I still don't know exactly what He wants from me. But I know He will tell me. As sure as I know that He will tell you."

"Well until He does I'm going to kick some ass in this land of our ancestors, and let those bastards know that they can steal our land and heritage but they'll never steal our pride!"

"Illa, you are too precious to hate so much." She used her cane to lift herself up from the chair and limp over to her daughter and began to caress her.

She still fought back the tears.

Later that evening Illapa walked near her mother's hut and leaned on a tree and thought about how bad it had been when she was small and her mother was drunk or high and men came over to her house at all hours of the day and night and her grandfather taking her to live with him and how she would run away back to her mother. She thought she could protect and help her back then. But she could not, and she wept back then for a father that abandoned them, the same way she finally lets some tears flow down her cheek, for the sorrow of her crippled mother and her dying grandfather who represented her past, her soul. She cried alone and bitter, with anger and vengeance in her heart.

The next Day.

She was surprised by the new emotions she was capable of provoking. When she thought of her grandfather, her love extended beyond religion. It was a faith in him and everything he was. As she sat next to his bed waiting for him to wake she scanned the room. She loved his old hat, so worn and weather-beaten as it hung on a rusty nail behind the wooden slatted door of his humble one room house. She reached out and took his alpaca poncho holding it tenderly to her face and inhaled his scent.

She walked about the room touching everything stopping every now and then when an object elicited a memory. She smiled and laid it gently as   she found it. When she had finished snooping she went to an old but inviting stuffed chair in one corner, sat in it and was asleep in minutes. She dreamed of Machu Pichu and her ancestors.

One moment they were riding in the modern Inca Train, the next they hiked on the highlands of the Inca Trail. Traveling across mountains and valleys always following the Urubamba River as it climbed along with them. The river was clear so it was the dry season but it suddenly turned dark and treacherous with a deluge of rains that went away as fast as they came. She dreamed on, going through the seasons in seconds.

They stopped among the many ruins along the river border and ate and caught naps, one second they were eating and camping by themselves the next they were guests of ancient Incas bringing them many delicacies to eat. Corn tortillas, roast guinea pig, mangos, chirimollas, and the plates kept coming. When they resumed their hike they were joined by several men and women all dressed in ancient regal splendor.

She slept soundly and dreamt in many colors which struck her as odd, she had never dreamt in color before.

Suddenly she was in the incredible main square of the Inca capital of Cuzco. She was being led by several monks. She was a child, no older than 5 or 6 years old. She was dressed in a raggedy poncho and her left hand was tied to another child in similar condition. The other child was also tied to another and she lost count of how many looking back at the long line. Some of them were younger and they were crying loudly. She went to a younger boy and hugged him   to her and he stopped crying.

In seconds she was surrounded by fine linens and clothing and an elegant lady was dressing her with fine European clothing. She felt safe and hugged the woman. She looked at the fine room, that turned into a church and she was kneeling in front of the altar inches away from the crucified Christ that was black like the night.

The shock of seeing the black face of Jesus and the strangeness of this ritual jolted her awake.

Her grandfather's face was inches from hers, he was nudging her.

"My sweet girl, I didn't mean to startle you, were you dreaming?"

"Yes, I had a weird and wonderful dream."

"Was I in your dream?" He said handing her a cup of steaming tea.

"Of course and some of our ancestors, and at the end I was...well I can't remember most of it." She lied, looking away.

"And what did our ancestors tell you, did you speak to them?"

"Yes, they fed us, and I think they were taking us to Machu Pichu, like in your stories. I also dreamt I was being raised by the Spanish in a fine home with an elegant lady, just like you told us."

"That is very interesting, what was her name?"

"How do I know, it was a dream." She teased him.

"It was Olga, Doña Olga de Quesada, she raised my mother when they found her living near Machu Pichu in the early part of this century. I remember visiting her when I was little boy. She was very kind. She left my mother a modest home and income when she died. I still live from some of the money. The Catholic Church arranged the trust fund. I didn't know it until I was a man. I found it strange, but then not all the Spaniards came to plunder and enslave, there were many good Christians among them."

He said wistfully taking her hand and leading her out of the house.

"I would like to see Machu Pichu one last time before I die, will you take me?"

Illapa did not hesitate.

"Of course grandfather, let's go today. We can talk along the way.

"Let's take your mother, she will love to go, I'm sure."

"All right, but it will be painful for her."

"It will be painful for all of us."

6

Cuzco and Machu Pichu, Peru a week later.

They rode into Cuzco at night to attract less attention, but the old man instructed their driver Luis, a devoted servant of Kusi Tupac the tribal leader, to drive around the main square first.

The incredible square came into view. The beautiful cathedral and the museum were lit by spotlights and glistened in the yellow hue casting a golden aura all around the façade of the main buildings. The colonial Spanish buildings that surrounded the square were fresh painted and their balconies polished. The city took pride in showing the   central square at its best.

If Cuzco was the capital of the mighty Incan Empire one wonders why there are no visible ruins in the center of the city. The explanation is simple. The Incan structures were so well built and their foundations solidly designed that the Spaniards built their cathedrals and buildings right on top of them. Underneath the great city's main square is the foundation designed and built by Incan craftsmen.

"Stop at the Cathedral Luis, we are getting out." The old man ordered the driver.

"Come, I want to show you something Illapa. Daughter stay with Luis, you can drive around the square perhaps you can stop where you can see us when we come out, we won't be long."

"Si señor."

The old man climbed the steps to the cathedral ignoring the two guards at the entrance. He reached back for Illapa and pushed open the massive wooden door, showing its age with pride.

They stepped inside the huge church and stopped to take in the grandeur of the place. They walked slowly to the main altar. "Wow", the girl whispered, enthralled at the ornate woodwork and opulence of the glistening altar.

"The silver for this altar came from Vilkabamba the Old, our richest silver processing center."

Illapa just gazed at the enormous altar and shook her head.

"The Spaniards used our own silversmiths to make it. Most of them had already converted; they worked the silver with love in their hearts for the one true God and his son the redeemer."

He looked at her wanting her to at the very least acknowledge his profound faith. She gave him a long look and offered nothing but an empty stare.

He smiled and led her by the arm to one of the many side chapels. They walked placidly towards the new altar with a crucified Christ looming above them.

Illapa's face contorted in amazement. The old man just pointed to the body of the savior and spoke softly.

"Have you ever seen a more beautiful Jesus? They say the wood was perfectly normal and light in color when they hung it in place. It turned with time. They say it's his way to show us he is one of us." He turned to his granddaughter and at last saw her expression and he felt her connection.

"Mi niña, you look as if you've seen a ghost." He was smiling.

"I...I can't believe it...I saw this Jesus in my dream, is this your magic grandfather? Have you put a spell on me?"

He laughed out loud in triumph.

"The only one who has that kind of magic is him. But we Christians don't call it magic; we call it faith, and miracles through Divine Intervention."

"I feel strange, very different...I mean physically...I'm a little dizzy. Something inside me is aching. I have this pressure in my chest and arms, grandfather...I'm...going to... faint..."

He reached for her as she was falling and caught her. He did his best to drag her over to a bench where he sat her down and let her lean on him. He stroked her hair and squeezed her arms and she slowly came back. She   looked at him with pleading eyes.

"Please get me out of here, I can't breathe." She pleaded.

He lifted her by placing his hand under her armpits and she regained some of her balance and footing. He escorted her to the door with his arm around her body helping her. Once outside the church he asked one of the guards, the Incan one for help. He came over and put his arms around her from the other side and together they helped her down the steps to the waiting car. The old man said it was nothing but the altitude and thanked the guard.

"Go with God my son." He told him.

"Mi niňa, mi niña what happened?"

"I'll be all right mother, just a little faint, let me just sit with the windows open, let's get out of here please."

"Vamos!" Said the old man.

Luis drove away slowly through the traffic not stopping until they reached a town not too far from Cuzco, where they stayed with a family that welcomed them like royalty. They bowed to the old man and treated the women with respect.

Illapa went to sleep as soon as her head hit the pillow.

At dawn the next day they started early for Aguas Calientes and Machu Pichu.

On The Road from Cuzco to Machu Pichu.

The ride from Cuzco is through a winding road that meanders across mountains and valleys and joins the Urubamba river. Then it runs alongside the riverbank for well over 100 kilometers.

The river is clear during the dry season and dark and treacherous when the rains come. As they drove they saw many ruins on its borders and mountain slopes. The very same ones Illapa had dreamt about. She smiled when she recognized some of the spots that were identical to what she remembered in her dream. Normally the tourists ride in buses that take them to a train station where they board the famous "Inka Train" that takes them parallel to the river to Aguas Calientes.

But Luis knew the winding dirt roads that were not comfortable for the tour buses and he drove over them at a steady clip making good time. No one blinked at the death-defying drop-offs inches from the tire tracks.

The old man slept most of the way along with her mother. Illapa tried to sleep but could only see her young mother drunk and high on drugs and she awoke with each attempt to find peaceful sleep.

She finally gave up and began to read Johan Reinhard's "The Nazca Lines: A new Perspective on their Origin and Meaning."

It was her grandfather's copy autographed by the author.

She remembered the many   times he was consulted by
foreigners and local scholars who came to see him from all corners
of the world when she was a little girl. They were always very kind
to her, bringing her presents. She liked the presents and attention
but she was always skeptical of their sincerity. Now reading their
words she reflected yet again on her grandfather as one of the last
remaining true Incas. And he would not be with her much longer.
She was not the only one that would miss him. Her nation and the
world would lose a link with their soul. Who would replace him,
in her heart? How could she connect again with her ancestors? She
was finally tired enough to sleep leaning on his shoulder.

The Town of Aguas Calientes.

They arrived in Aguas Calientes just in time for breakfast.
Luis drove slowly avoiding the early morning tourists making
their way from the Inka Train Station. He drove without stopping
to the end of the short main road almost to the point where the
road climbed steeply into the mountains. He pulled up to a small
stall with rustic wooden tables out front that only had a few
patrons and they were all Incan. The owner came out when he saw
him and ushered all of them inside to a comfortable table and
served them himself.

Illapa excused herself and went out for a walk. She walked
down to the main section of the small town and sat at a concrete
break wall next to the Urubamba and watched the rapids twenty
feet below her. The water was high and cloudy due to recent rains.

The splash of the flow creating   foamy   collisions   with   the
smooth rocks. The angry river roared by and made a turn about a
quarter mile and climbed slightly through a fertile valley
surrounded by plush green mountains on either side. On her left
was a small patch of dirt with some flowers and she recognized the
familiar "Wakanki" as well as the well known Peruvian Poinsettias
with their bright red bracts resembling petals.

Two handsome tourists came up the walk and stopped to
talk to her.

"Buenos Dias señorita." The taller, heavier one said to her in
a heavy accent.

Americans she presumed.

The big guy wore a Miami Dolphins jacket over faded blue
jeans and the perfunctory Reeboks. The smaller man just wore a
heavy flannel plaid shirt with a burgundy fleece vest, he wore
black jeans and leather boots.

"Good Morning." She replied in perfect English.

"Ah, good you speak American."

"Where can we get a good breakfast before we head to
Machu Pichu, something to hold us for the day so that we don't
lose steam in the ruins?" Asked the smaller of the two in a thick
southern drawl.

She smiled politely.

"Well you can go across the street to that tourist trap and fill
up on eggs and bacon and coffee. Or you can walk a few more
blocks to the end of the road and look for a small stall called El
Condor where they will serve you an authentic Peruvian breakfast

for half the price. And don't   forget the Coka Tea for the altitude."

"Oh we take altitude pills, we don't need any tea."

She smiled politely.

"You guys are ready to go then, enjoy the ruins."

"Hey you wouldn't want to join us for the day; we are going to need a guide, how about it." The big guy looked at her lustfully.

"No thank you, I'm here with my family, you will find plenty of great guides at the entrance. I highly recommend a guide to tell you all about the things that are not in the brochures and point out the important facts about our Sacred Center."

"You see, I knew you were one of them, come on you can do it if you really want. Isn't there something I can do to convince you?"

The big guy crossed the line; he held out a wad of bills and tried to touch her left breast.

His hand reached to within an inch of her left nipple when she took his hand and bent it back and in one motion leaped off the bench at the same time produced a short commando blade concealed on her belt that she placed across his jugular.

The younger man jumped away in fear.

"Holy Shit!" was all he said

"Now "Rambo", you still want to grab my breast? Because if you do it will be the last thing your filthy hands feel on this earth! Comprende!"

"Yes." He said meekly.

"What was that, I didn't   hear you?"

"Yes, mam...please don't hurt me...please" he pleaded almost in tears.

"Ok, then. Go and enjoy the day. But stay away from my sisters?"

"Yes, Yes."

She pushed him away and walked across the street. Her grandfather was waiting for her on the opposite sidewalk, he was shaking his head sternly, but there was a hint of a proud grin on his lips.

The Road to Machu Pichu.

The two thousand foot climb up the mountain from Aguas Calientes to the magic city is an interesting zigzag trail over mostly unpaved roads alongside a mountain with no guard-rail to help if you slip off the side into the precipice high over the Urubamba River below.

The last time the old man had visited his great city he had done it on foot hiking up the Inka trail. He was a spry 65 then making the 43 km trek with no problems. The trail was originally laid with large precise "tiles" of white granite carved out of the mountainside. The Inka trail, like everything they built, was done meticulously and with functionality rivaling anything built by modern craftsmen.

When they reached the entrance Luis drove to a corner of the small parking area. He waved to one of the attendants and he sauntered over waving him off   not to park. Luis parked and got out of the car and spoke to him softly, they both looked over to the back seat and the old man waved to them. The attendant nodded and took the car keys. Luis then came over and ushered them towards the Park entrance. The attendant excused himself between Illapa and Luis and knelt at old man's feet. He was quickly helped up by Luis who thanked him again and gave him twenty soles, but he would not take them. He backed away and took the car to a safe parking area.

Luis went to the ticket booth and purchased their entrance fees. They were not accosted by any of the numerous guides. They all recognized and acknowledged a true Inka among their midst.

Once inside they made their way slowly towards the city.

"Grandfather, did you see all those tourists getting their passports stamped. Everyone wants a piece of our history."

"Yes, wouldn't you?"

"You know what I mean why do they come here? What is it that they all want? Do they all expect to be enlightened?"

"I rather think it's as simple as wanting to feel something spiritual, something remarkable. This is no cushy beach vacation; this in many ways is a pilgrimage. But not in the religious way, more in a discovery, a quest for meaning in our lives."

"Hmmm. I don't know if I buy that, some of these "pilgrims" don't seem to have much in the brain-cage. I think all they want is to see an alien or cave painting and to send a picture back home to O-HI-O and say *look what we did*, we climbed a mountain in quaint Peru!"

"My child, don't be so   judgmental, I'm sure there are some as you say, but I like to think that no matter why they come our magic city enthralls and makes most of them think."

She looked at him and smiled a granddaughter's smile of approval.

And then they finally came to the point where the city came into view. They all looked at their heritage as if for the first time.

To a first time visitor one cannot imagine how they built it so high in the mountains way back in the fifteenth century.

To Illapa a modern woman member of the visual television generation it always hit her that the whole city seemed like an elaborate movie set. Such a precise design, with open plazas, hanging gardens, neat row houses, pavilions and altars for entertainment and don't forget the observatory.

They climbed and descended slowly so as not to overwhelm the old man. After a short hike they reached The Temple of the Three Windows and sat down to rest and eat some of the snacks that Luis produced from his back pack.

"Grandfather, tell us again how you told Bingham[1] to leave our city alone and let it lie beneath its cover of vegetation?"

"But only you revered leader direct descendant of Pachacuti could have told Bingham how our city was to be treated, tell us please what you told him?" Luis pleaded with him.

"I tried to tell him about our ancestors and specifically of the Inca Yupanqui, but all he wanted was his so-called "secrets" of Machu Pichu. I tried to tell him there were no secrets. And if there were and I told him, well, then they would not be secrets anymore, would they?" He smiled that   knowing   smile   that   spoke volumes not about what he was saying but what he was NOT saying.

"He came to me because he found my aunts working the land, they told him he would have to talk to me. I don't know why, I was just a young man when he finally found me. But I told him what my father told me and his father told him. No-one outside the Inca nation is to have knowledge of Machu Picchu, no one is to have the keys to our Kingdom."

"You know the story I get tired of telling it, it matters not in the overall scheme of things as they turned out." The old man looked away.

"But grandfather they have said so many things about our city, don't you want to set the record straight. Don't you want to tell them how great we were?"

"That's the point granddaughter, "WERE!", we are no longer the once and mighty empire. We are a conquered people. We have blended into modern society. Whether right or wrong is for God to decide. As far as our secrets they will die with us. I will pass them on to you before I die. And you will pass them on to your children. And that is all I have to say about Bingham and my city."

The old man walked over to a bush next to the third window, Peru's national bird, cock-of-the rock, a dazzling bird native to the magic city, had perched on one of the branches. The old man held out his hand, palm down, to the colorful male. He shook his brilliant bright-orange head and appeared to look around before gingerly stepping on to the offered perch. He gently raised the bird in front of his face for all to see and reached up with his other hand and stroked his head.

To the amazement of all, the large bird acted as if he knew him.

He brought his lips close to the brilliant plumage and whispered some words and smiled.

They all watched in awe and smiled with him.

7

Lima, Peru March 1997

It was the third month of the siege on the Japanese Ambassador's home in Lima Peru.

Illapa and her new lover Marcos, a tall handsome man almost twice her age and a high ranking member of the Tupac Amaru Revolutionary Movement (MRTA) [2] were walking up the stairs to the second floor living quarters, he was behind her patting her ass. She was playing her coy role, accepting his advances then slapping his hand away.

He persisted, finally grabbing her around the waist and kissing her neck and her hair that she kept well hidden under the skull mask. She allowed his advances. She wanted the sexual release as much as he did. Once on the second floor they made their way to one of the bedrooms belonging to one of the children of the ambassador.

He was now kissing her passionately but she was not responding. She did not like to kiss her lovers, for kissing was more intimate and she had not kissed any man intimately. She pulled her face away and pushed him on the bed. She unbuckled his belt and pulled down his pants. She put her mouth where a man will not resist the pleasure and where for her it was just a physical way to control men. When his moans grew louder she climbed on top of him and finished in total control.

"Wow!" he said exhausted.

"We better get back." She told him, dressing quickly and walking out of the room.

Downstairs in the rear of the home a headquarters had been set up. She heard loud arguments. Marcos walked by her and went into the room. She went to her assigned post and napped until it was time for her watch.

Marcos had recruited her for the MRTA when Javier, who still worshipped her and stayed in touch with her, had introduced them in Cuzco. She had said yes without hesitating. Anything to get back in the game, she thought back then

During her guard duty, Panchito, a young student from Lima who had befriended her even though Illapa treated him with cool disdain, came and sat with her.

"I can't stand that Marcos. He's a pig!" He looked in disgust at Illapa.

Illapa knew the details. Female guerrillas would have sex with the leaders almost on demand. She hated it but resigned herself to doing it for the "cause".

"Hey at least you like him," He added, emphasizing the point to Illapa.

"I hate his fucking guts, I can't stand him. I take what I want from him and give him what I want, period." She replied.

"He sure likes you, or else he would not have allowed you join us as the only woman."

"He likes any woman who spreads her legs. The man is a stinking whore. And he's rich too, comes from a wealthy family.

The very ones we are trying to destroy. Go figure. I will be damn glad when this whole thing is over and done with."

"Do you think this will end well, will they give in to our demands?"

"I think this whole operation is a fuck-up from day one."

The young man looked at Illapa and thought long and hard about what she just said.

They missed an opportunity to capture the U.S. Ambassador to Peru, who was turned away at the gate when the attack began. They released the man that would become the future president of Peru. And most   important they released the mother of their most hated antagonist President Fujimori[3].

They had made many mistakes. It would all come out in the end.

8

The siege would last 126 days. Towards the end Illapa sensed that this was going not going to end well. Conventional and unconventional wisdom declare one must never live for another, that one must only live for oneself. We are born alone and alone we will die. But there is no joy here…there is only apprehension. It was a nightmare that she wanted to end. The siege and her angst. No point in living. What did she live for?

These questions without answers, these sins were a cumbersome weight to carry on her young shoulders. Although

she did not believe in God, she   did   not   fear   death.
Complacency and mediocrity was what she feared more. She had
faced death many times in her short life and it did not look half-
bad. She just wanted to get on with the next chapter.

On the final day she went up to the same second floor
bedroom where she always went to find silence. While in the
bedroom she felt an overwhelming peace. She was glad all of a
sudden, glad and peaceful. She felt as if she shouldn't be there. It
was not good. Everything around her was in slow motion. She
knew what her job was; her attitude had always been fixed and
true. Yet, here she was taking a mind break, a pause to think and
reflect. She moved softly towards a beautiful painting of a sunrise
in a Japanese bay. The sun's rays seemed to glitter in the sea. She
had glanced at the painting many times, but this time she saw it for
the first time. It was splendid. And then when she turned away
from the painting, she stood face to face with a wooden cross, the
ones made by artisans in the street markets. She felt a connection,
she slowly brought her hand to her forehead and instinctively and
without thought, she traced the cross, from head to her chest, to
her heart, and to her right breast. She heard herself whisper, "God
help me."

She opened the door and walked into the closet and began
to look around. She pulled out a pink evening gown and held it
against her figure. She came out of the closet, took off her
masculine terrorist uniform and when she was naked she placed
the dress in front of her body and twirled around like a teenager
preening for Prom. She slipped into the dress and it seemed to fit

her small figure very well. She   looked at herself in the mirror and smiled; she let her long hair loose and shook it free, a new woman smiled back.

That was the last thing she remembered before the force of the explosion sent her into unconsciousness.

The raid was carried out meticulously and with precision. Military trained commandos had months to prepare. They cut down the MRTA insurgents before they could harm the hostages. The entire MRTA unit was killed. Panchito had been killed instantly when an explosion blew the door he was guarding. There were reports of mutilations and assassinations but all the rumors were squashed by the overwhelming success and support for President Fujimori, who took personal credit for the entire operation. It was reported that all the guerrillas were males and all were accounted for.

Illapa regained consciousness in a hospital bed a few hours later. Except for a few minor cuts and bruises, she was fine. Her head ached, and she figured she had a concussion.

The hospital was a mad house with activity. People screaming in pain, doctors and nurses moving swiftly about.

An Incan nurse was the first thing she saw when her eyes focused. She was standing over her wiping her face with a sponge that felt like heaven on her face. The nurse would wipe the dust from her skin that had given her a pale almost white complexion like the face in the paintings of the great Virgin Queen Elizabeth. The nurse wiped her face and hair and squeezed the sponge clean in a bowl that she had placed on the bed next to her patient. It took several minutes for her to complete her job. She stood back and gasped.

"Oh my God! You are Incan, we thought you were Japanese."

By this time Illapa had regained most of her wits.

"My sister please don't be alarmed I need to go look for my family can you please help me find them?"

The older woman nodded meekly.

Illapa reached up and touched the woman's face and then lowered her hand to the top button of her uniform and began to undo it. The older woman began to cry softly.

"Shhhhh." She whispered soothingly. "We are going to change clothes, then I'm going to walk out of here and you are going to get into this bed and stay very quiet for fifteen minutes, then you can do whatever you want. Ok?"

The woman nodded slowly her puzzled look turning into one of fear.

She changed quickly into the nurse's uniform and rolled her hair under the nurse's cap. She then turned to the nurse lying on the bed in her underwear and covered her with the sheet and whispered, "My sister please stay quiet for a few minutes and give me a chance to live," she deliberated, "I mean I don't want to cause any harm to anyone, especially you."

Why did she say "live"? She only reflected for an instant then she walked out into the Hospital corridor and walked confidently without stopping out the emergency entrance past the soldiers and families and walked into the city streets.

She found some money in   the woman's pocket and hailed a taxi.

"Where to nurse?"

She thought for a moment and gave him the address to Javier's house. He had not participated in the MRTA attack out of fear, or perhaps conscience. When Illapa arrived he hugged her and was very glad to see her alive.

In the uproar of the military success her escape was kept secret by the government. But within hours Javier confronted her with the inevitable truth.

"Mi niña, you have to leave Lima and probably Peru. They are hunting you down and they will find you and kill you or worse, make you a spectacle for their propaganda bullshit. You must leave." He said to her.

"And where do you propose I go?"

"Go north out of Peru and hide in the mountains with the Indians. I have a friend that can get you to Cuzco and from there his contacts will get you to the mountains."

"I would have rather died with my comrades."

"No, you don't really believe that."

"No I don't, in the end I wanted to get out, something came over me the day of the raid, I don't know what it was, all I know is I did not want to kill or be killed."

"Of course you want to live, why would you want to die?"

"For a long time I wanted to die, to die for my people, fighting for truth and justice. And now, now I don't know who I am… or what I want. All I know is I want to live."

"Thank God." He said   adding. "I will make the arrangements to leave immediately."

"Yes, I think God had something to do with it." She said softly.

Linda

"The lust for comfort murders the passions of the soul."

-Khalil Gibran, mystic, poet, and artist

9

Miami, Florida 1993

The alarm goes off at 6:30 am. It is one of those modern digital types that sound like some sort of techno bird's resonant call. It is really quite unbearable. Quickly but clumsily her small delicate hand presses the "snooze" button and there is quiet again, for at least a seven minute interval. Then it goes off again. The same hand, less clumsily this time, presses the button again.

It is 7:12 before the young woman finally reaches for the "off" switch and permanently silences the obstinate noise.

Even in her drowsy state she is absolutely beautiful.

She finally wakes up. A perfect caricature of today's woman. Tall, voluptuous with perfect medium sized round firm breasts, slim trim waist, and   wide erotic hips. Every man's fantasy and most women's nightmare. She wanted children by now but a busy life held them back. Perhaps when this entire crisis blows over they can start the family they both crave.

She wants so much out of life. Too smart to waste in some legal steno pool. Soon she will do more. Ambition drives her. Love fuels her passion to succeed. She wants to go to law school and have babies. Somehow the two are like oil and water. No matter; she will do it. She will bubble with excitement as she tells you that she is the wave of the future, and how she wants to be involved in something that will help shape humanity.

But why did she marry Alejandro Dionisio Garcia?

Linda Garcia! She thought it was cute. She used to flaunt her new name when they were newlyweds five years ago. But now when people ask or look indiscreetly she politely explains how she married this Cuban guy. But she really loves Alex, she cannot help herself, he is so gorgeous. Her "Latin-lover", she tells her girlfriends. She truly loves him, his family and all that went with it.

Alex's father's death was a shock for her. She had grown close and very fond of the old man. She learned to love and admire "Don Pepe", and the way he would take her side in their family arguments. When she became fluent in Spanish, Don Pepe came to her and they lovingly spent one rainy afternoon reading the poetry of Marti and Neruda together. She especially enjoyed his own romantic verses, the ones he had not published for their personal content, some with   sensual erotic overtones. She especially loved the one he had written for his beloved wife when she first refused his advances but saved his eternal soul by bringing him back to the Church. He called it "My Passion".

"I thank you for my soul, my love
I came within a breath of losing all
Raising the devil's curtain on our stage
Softly unveiling the proscenium
From where I stood exposed under the lights, trembling
Against the cold, grey breath of death
Penitent, screaming to the Lord.
Oh! How we strain our lifeline
When we clutch the weight of sin."

She had wonderful erotic fantasies involving her father-in-law. Always he was her older distinguished lover. God how she loved the kisses, the experienced caresses, they seemed so real. She did not feel guilt. She was definitely not ashamed of loving him that way. Besides, she knew they were dreams, sexual fantasies that satisfied her and made her glow.

Alex laughed out loud and teased her when she confided in him with some of the details. He told her she had the "hots" for the old man. She knew better. Jose Manuel Garcia was a very romantic man. A man, she knew, that would love you entirely and reach into your soul, touch your heart and fulfill your dreams.

When she first heard the news, it was too much for her to

bear. She had collapsed in a   heap in front of the family. Not Alex nor her father would ever understand the special sorrow she felt.

When her own father and stepmother had come to her bedside she had to invent a story about being under emotional strain at work and school, and that the death of Don Pepe was just the trigger of her breakdown. She just could not bring herself to tell them what he had meant to her. She took pity on her parents. They were not like him. They were cold and unsentimental like she had been before she joined her new family. Besides they never really approved of her marriage.

"You are so young!" They had preached the same sermon that all young lovers hear; "you still do not know what you want." It came out cold and detached an edict without emotion or sentiment ushered from an Ice Palace directed at unruly subjects.

"Screw them!" She had said to Alex. She was in the middle of college, her head filled with rebellious wonder rather than fear of the future. She eloped with Alex, and thrilled at the thought of having married the handsome son of a famous Cuban poet and leader.

They had roamed the country the first two years of their marriage. They went with Don Pepe and his entourage every chance they could as he made his way across all the pockets where Cuban-Americans had settled. Places like New York and New Jersey, Chicago, L.A. and a small but highly vocal community in Austin, Texas where they enjoyed the warmth of Don Pepe's closest friend, Dr. Abelardo Ruiz and his large close knit family.

When Alex decided to get a master's degree, The University of Texas in Austin was the logical choice. So Linda said goodbye to her family and followed her husband to Texas for two years.

Austin became the second headquarters of Don Pepe, as well as his retreat from the grind of public life. Here amidst the smell of "sofrito" the clicking of dominoes and the loud boisterous voices of the people that surrounded them they all became part of "La Causa", the struggle for freedom for their homeland. Linda lived, felt, hated, and loved every moment of the experience. And she quickly belonged like all of them. Under the guidance of Don Pepe the people responded. It had been a long time since someone had picked up the banner and united them. Very few men and women emerge as true leaders. The people expect too much from them. Cubans demand that their leader must be well above usual. He must be different, brave, talented, loud, humorous, strong and most important, he must love his country and his people with fanatical spirit and pride. Jose Manuel Garcia was all that and a poet, like the Cuban liberator Jose Marti.

Everywhere they went Linda specially sensed a profound admiration and respect for the old man. Even his opponents respected him. Don Pepe they called him. Some disagreed with him but they all listened. His words moved them. The simplicity of his views scared the intellectuals and the "old guard" politicians. His easy manner and poetic style took in the vast majority of the disenfranchised exiles.

Linda could see his magnetic character draw them in to "La

Causa". "The Cause".

And in the small intervals between the travel and speeches he read poetry and took them to far out wonderful places to eat the most exotic food and drink he could find. He was fond of tasting something for the first time, a local beer or a good aged cheese. She cherished those memories and the warm loving feeling they brought.

How could she explain all this to her father! She never had to discuss any of this new life to him. When she and Alex finally returned to Miami, Mark was close to suicide. It was Linda's turn to save her father. With the help of Alex and Don Pepe and the rest of the now rather large extended family she gradually helped him find a new meaning.

And now Don Pepe was gone. What would she do? Alex alone could not fill the void, the need, the love!

Her father had come back into her life with a new caring and warmth that had given her hope through these difficult times. She was growing closer to him. She now needed him and he was there for her. Alex was depressed and distant and she was not able to break through. She was so tired, so sick and tired.

She went to the bathroom to wash. From the smell of his cologne she realized he had gotten up early and had gone out. It did not surprise her. He had done it before. Recently he had taken to going out late or leaving very early. She saw him stand on the edge of the beach for hours at a time. He walked the shoreline for miles, refusing her company, hardly speaking to her. She asked him to go to church with her, the look he gave her sent a cold chill

down here spine. Lovemaking   became desultory and lacking
his usual passion. She thought it would pass in time. She stood by
him.   When he took a leave of absence from his position at the
bank, she counseled against it.   "The worst thing you could do,"
she pleaded with him,"you have to keep busy, to do something to
keep your mind from wandering." She was worried for him. His
emotions had changed to a detached coldness.   "Please tell me
what to do," she begged through tears, "You cannot go on like
this".   "Let's have a baby, now would be good for us to bring a
new life a new beginning into our lives." She would never forget
the look in his eyes that day she mentioned the baby. He looked at
her through a new face. She felt fear for the first time in her life. He
changed quickly and spoke in a calm self-assured tone;
"everything will be all-right very soon."   She believed him and
sensed a change in him.

She washed the sleep from her face and as she placed the
soap in the soapdish she noticed the missing razor and shaving kit.
She hastily inspected the cabinet. Most of his things were gone.
Startled, she made her way to her dresser where she found the
note. She read it twice.

She cried softly. The strained new tears flowed, slowly,
quietly conquering every inch of her beautiful face as she wept
sitting naked on the edge of the bed.

10

Miami, Florida 1995

Mark Francis Russo lived the good life. He lived in a Spanish hacienda style home in "the City Beautiful", Coral Gables. An area of plush refurbished homes with lots of character and charm. Great schools and snobs for neighbors. But he surely deserved the good life. He came from a large Italian family from the coal belt of Pennsylvania. The coal dust and freezing cold weather had convinced him early in his manhood that there had to be a better   life. One year when his father finally scraped up enough money from his job in the railroad serving the coal mines, he piled the family in an old station wagon and drove south.

A winter vacation was the reality of the wealthy but his father dreamed big. In the warm south, particularly Miami, he found his paradise.   Mark was only in his mid teens, but he promised himself right then and there overlooking the Atlantic Ocean on the sands of what would one day become the famous South Beach, that he would make South Florida his home.

He awoke early every morning, to drag his sleep-drugged body around the house turning off the burglar alarms. He really did not want them, but they were a gift, or at least that was what justified the influence-peddling from the president of the largest private protection agency in the world.

He looked in the mirror at the tired but handsome face. A blond blue-eyed Sicilian not quite six feet tall. He patted his stomach examining his new "washboard abs", well, at least a semblance of one or two. Finally, he stood on the scale. Today was a good day, down three pounds; 193. His body was in much better shape than ten years ago. At 56, he was a young middle-aged father of three kids under the age of ten. A second family, a final hope at happiness.

He walked around the house in the quiet of the early morning and headed for the indoor heated pool. He plunged into the water and began his morning swim, an active and vibrant human being. He had to be to keep up with the city. After he became State Attorney for Miami-Dade County two years ago it seemed that he was always on the run.

"Dealing with crime, the politicians, a million Cuban-Americans as well as thousands of other assorted immigrants, is no picnic!" he always told his critics.

But he did his job well and the critics were few. He was a tough boss, but a fair one, respected and well liked by the rank and file. He mingled with the minorities and the Cubans. He got along with them. He felt he knew them.

After the swim he dressed quickly. He wanted to be early today.

Before leaving the bedroom he woke his wife Connie. He told her to water the roses early, that it would be a hot day. Then he kissed her as she mumbled the words she always said when they parted, "God be with you."

He did not go in the boy's room. They would be asleep. He went to his daughter's bedroom door and knocked gently.

"Is that you, Dad?" said a sweet voice.

"If you want a ride with me today you had better hurry, I am leaving early."

"OK, I'll be down in two shakes, please wait."

He smiled; he was pleased that she rode with him most mornings.

Linda was going to law school, and he loved the chance to talk to her first thing in the morning. She was the sunshine that warmed his world; the day would start a little better because of her presence sitting along side him in the car.

The day she announced   to the family and some close friends over dinner that she was going to law school was one of his fondest and proudest moments. She was getting on with her life; he would help her as she had helped him.

He went out of the house and fussed with his roses. This year would be good. The fresh topsoil he brought down from Pennsylvania would do the trick. The Rose Fair was still three months away. His hopes were high.

Mark loved gardening. The roses were his pride and joy. For a man who lived with turmoil and violence every day of his life, it was an unusual calling. But not illogical. His love for the earth and the beautiful roses was a perfect metaphor for the ugly stigma of crime and man's inhumanity to man. It was an escape and a sedative from reality. He tilled and worked the soil and planted and nurtured the seeds. He researched new fertilizers and soils for his garden was the best on his block, and that's what he believed.

At work he built a reputation as an innovator and motivator. Traveling the world in search of the latest crime fighting techniques. His special tactics team was his pride and joy. One of the best in the world. The pride he felt was a direct result of the amount of time, effort and caring that he put into his work and once more into his own life. Once more his life had structure and meaning. A purpose to live, achieve and lead. He had lost this once, he cherished it now.

Linda Marie Russo swept out of the front door of the house as if strutting into a courtroom. Suitcase in one hand, a bundle of files in the other and golden hair swaying around her beautiful face.

"They really look good". She said as she arranged herself on the front seat of the bland Chevrolet Impala the county provided to her father. Linda did not do much gardening. But she loved the way Mark arranged his garden, especially the roses. She often picked some of the best to take with her to school. When her father caught her she always made him smile: "But Daddy they will remind me of you all day!"

He started out weaving through the maze of empty side streets avoiding the crowds. She smiled at him the same smile every time, forever accepting this idiosyncrasy.

Once he was on a main road he turned to her as she was just finishing the last touches of her make-up.

She smiled at him invitingly.

"You are ravishing". He obliged.

"You are biased". She said, pleasantly beaming.

Mark grinned enjoying the moment. Linda replaced all the tools of beauty and began casually. "You have your job cut out for you today!"

"Yeah"

"What time will the President be here?" She let the question hang not really expecting an answer. She was thinking about the Stiltsville tort and Professor Howsler.

Linda kissed his cheek before leaving him. She walked swiftly and disappeared around a building. Mark grinned. That wonderful feeling of pride and admiration filled him again. She had waved quickly struggling   with her load, but she always waved like the wings of a dove, softly reaching him and sending him over the edge. His eyes watered and just so gently overran the damn of his lid and a single tear flowed down his face. He was not an emotional man. But every once in awhile they came, the tears. He accepted them, he knew them. They were part of her and the special bond they shared.

He loved her more today, more than when she was that little bundle of curls with the challenging attitude. She was a tough little girl, very attached to her mother. How he missed seeing them together. He wished her mother could see her now. He somehow hoped she could.

Like him, his beloved Rose would have been amazed at her maturity in the face of adversity. To see her bloom, like his precious roses, to the beautiful flower she was. How much she had endured. The turmoil of her marriage. It seemed as is no one understood, even he could not understand. He tried, but it was all so bizarre. Linda had gone through the ringer.

He had liked Alex from the beginning. He merely gave them a hard time playing the dutiful father. He wished he had not hidden his true feelings back then. There were enough lies in their lives and he was now ashamed. He had confronted Alex to tell him, but it was too late. He saw it in his eyes; he felt the coldness, the detached look. He knew it well. He had seen it a few times in the faces of the most hideous serial killers that he had come across. He was afraid for Linda, and told her so. She angrily defended her husband and his tortured past.

Mark remembered the arguments well. He had talked down at her then, not to her. She stood her ground. He tried to slap her once. She stood firm awaiting the blow. He could not do it. He was glad. Now he understood. Linda was special. Now he saw it clearly. He often wondered if she felt the same. He took comfort in the thought she did.

Mark looked back rarely. But today was a good day for melancholy and laments. He knew the futility of reliving the past. He had crossed that bridge. He had a new life. A good life. The pain had given way to a new confident resolve. There was a ruling structure to his existence. He looked at things in a new way. It had taken him a long time. But as he drove through the crowded streets of Little Havana and gazed out at the faces of the city, he felt good. He knew in his heart that he was fortunate. He was beginning to understand the world around him, the good and the bad and the vast middle of life. He was mellowing. The scars of life were there, he felt them now and then, but the pain had faded and what remained was wisdom and peace.

It was his wife Rose's courageous battle against cancer and her slow painful death. *The horror of it all.* She had been so fragile all of her life. He sometimes felt like her older brother and not her husband. She had needed him and his strength; he was her crutch, lending his hand, giving her courage. But it was not enough. Linda was her gift and her blessing. Rose never told him about the pregnancy until it was too late to do anything about it. He did not want to drain her strength with the burden of childbirth.

She went ahead and had Linda. Rose died when Linda was twelve. They were very close all the short time they had together. Linda helped take care of her mother and after she died she took care of her father until he married Connie.

Concetta Theresa Russo could not ever begin to fill the hole in Linda's heart after her mother died. She was an independent self-sufficient woman with towering strength. She did not need Linda's help, nor Mark's. She did not need them like Rose. Connie spent the first five years of her marriage to Mark trying to prove her love. She finally gave up and dedicated herself to making a good home for them and concentrating on bringing up her children.

Connie almost destroyed Mark with love. She made his house a model of the middle class. Everything was structured and planned with a purpose and goal. She would cook wonderful gourmet meals from fancy books. She showered him with presents of jewelry. Mark never liked jewelry before. She thanked him constantly for her life and home and the family she had always envisioned. She would discuss everything with him, boring him incessantly. Of course, she could not realize he couldn't care less because he was buried in the beaurocratic humdrum of the Dade County Public Safety Department of Minority Relations. He was about to hit fifty and began to question his life and happiness. He began an affair with a scandalous young Cuban woman in his office. He also became a regular at Tobacco Road, a wonderful watering hole with the oldest liquor license in the City nestled by the Miami River and the government offices. His drinking became a problem just after his mistress lied to him when she told him she was pregnant. All she wanted was to lure him away from his family. Then Linda announced her love for Alex and when he went ballistic and acted like an idiot she eloped with him. She was barely 19!

He lost it. He came crashing down into the void of despair. He became a cliché. A member of society's middle class disenchanted nothings. His life was in the toilet. He lacked substance, structure and meaning. He drifted from day to day. From the nightmares to the painful agonizing hangovers.

At the bottom, he reached out to the only person that could help him. And she was there for him. The rescue and reunion was subdued, but in their eyes they saw the spark of life. The glimmer of light and day. The love of parent and child. When a parent helps a child no matter how old there is love and gladness. But when a child helps a parent, no matter what age, there is magic…tears…blessings!

Linda spent hours with him. Nursing him, babying him, scolding him. Healing his wounds, real and imaginary. She brought him into her new family. She took care of Connie. Counseling her to give him some room. As her new Cuban family celebrated life with their wonderful music, food and customs she carefully exposed her father to the healing force of love of family and friends.

Slowly Mark responded.

One day in a drunken binge he had wallowed for days watching old sentimental movies and then he found Don Pepe's book of poetry and read "My Passion". He understood at last how big the hole in his heart was. How he needed to fill it with something new. He went to a church and found a priest to whom he confessed his sins. Slowly at first he found his way back to the faith of his family. His spiritual life was reborn and he felt the redeeming power of love.

Alexander

"A thing is not necessarily true because a man dies for it."

-Oscar Wilde, author, playwright

11

Port of Spain, Trinidad and Tobago, 1998

Alex recognized Mohan from the dossier. He was well briefed by Martica Vega on the trip to Trinidad. He did not disclose to her that he had been here before when he was a banker. So when she hinted that he would feel like he was in India or Pakistan and not the Caribbean, he asked her why even though he knew. You will see was all she said. He remembered then how she led him to her bedroom and without saying a word began to undress casually. When Martica was naked she walked over to him and helped him with his clothes. They went at it like two animals in heat. This was not lovemaking it was sex. Alex needed it and so did she. Afterwards they fell asleep facing away from each other as if nothing had happened.

Mohan waved at him first. "Alex, please…yes?" he said in a caribbean east Indian flair.

"Yes, Mohanlal Ramutarsingh?"

"Call me Mohan"

They shook hands.

"Please to give me your papers and I will expedite your entry."

Alex followed him to the front of the customs desk where Mohan handed the papers and passport to an older man who studied them carefully and stamped them.

Behind the customs agent stood another man whose uncomfortable gaze never left him as he walked by the crowded customs area. He was darker than Mohan with jet-black very straight hair well combed with a keen shine. He was dressed in a white guayabera...the business suit of the Caribbean, a cotton dress shirt common to the tropics. The starched whiteness of the shirt accentuated his blackness.

Mohan's features were starkly different. He remembered from his previous visit the different racial strains on the island. He would get very good at recognizing the Hindus from the Muslims and even some of the classes and sects within each. Mohan was Hindu and the customs clerk was Muslim; two very diverse beliefs sharing one Caribbean island thousands of miles from their roots. Both now part of a different land, a tropical one. And Trinidad was just 15 miles from Venezuela and the South American mainland.

The Next Morning.

Alex walked out of the "Upside-down Hilton in Port of Spain. It was late morning. He had just under an hour to kill before his lunch date. He smiled at his surroundings. Who would have thought he would be living in the heart of this strange and bustling capital of Trinidad among the milieu of cultures. The Hilton was built in the sixties alongside a hill overlooking the heart of Port of Spain. The lobby was on the top of the hill and thus you made your way down to the rooms and hence its name. From its open walkways and balconies one could see as far as the port and the oil tankers anchored waiting to load their crude.

After making contact with the militant underground in Miami through his friend and lover he had been sent to Trinidad to await instructions.

He killed time walking to the central park just a few blocks away and drinking coconut water sold by the peddlers, and watching cricket matches. Even though he could not follow the complicated game, he marveled at the graceful "pitching" and "batting". It seemed so familiar to his beloved baseball, but the scoring was impossible to understand.

A couple of times he ventured out to Maracas Bay to swim at the only decent beach on the island. A visitor to Trinidad soon discovers that unless you venture to Tobago, the other island that makes up the country, you will not see the Caribbean island we all have in mind, with miles of white sand beaches and resorts. The island of Trinidad is one huge oil town. It has the main campus of the University of the West Indies and the best airport in the Caribbean. But as far as   tourism even the locals go to Barbados on their vacation.

His neighbor across the hall was from Peru; a land of mystery and magic. He engaged the cultured old man in long conversations even though he was told not to socialize with anyone. His new identity was safe for the moment. The harmless and charming old man was a descendant of the Incas. He was desperate for conversation and Alex invited him to an early breakfast one morning, where the old man talked and talked, recanting stories of the Incan way of life and their beliefs. Having visited Lima on a short business trip a few years back, the land and its people fascinated Alex. He had always wanted to go back and visit the city of Cuzco and Machu Pichu in the Andes.

The old man was very short and thin. He appeared frail but there was a wiry sinewy strength to his whole body that assured Alex he was a healthy man even for his age, which he offered cheerfully as 88 years old. His face was naturally suntanned bronze in color.

His hair, very thin and straight, once was jet black he bragged, and down to his waist in his younger days. Now it was white. A pure bright white like the fine linen napkins on the table, it was cut neatly around his collar. His eyes were still dark and alive, surrounded by wonderful wrinkles that grew in number when he smiled. His nose was a little too big for his face, but it set up the eyes above it nicely. His mouth was small, with thin lips the color of ripe plums. Sometimes Alex would picture him with all the plumes, headdress and gold of a pre-Columbian

Inca Chief and the picture was   a colorful and pleasant one. He shared his thoughts with the old man, eliciting a Mona Lisa smile.

He had left the old man in his room reading the latest edition of the Lima Herald earlier and now as he stepped into the light and heat of the tropical morning, his thoughts turned to the man he was about to meet.

He walked the two blocks to the park like any other day. Alex looked around him and at first very slowly he seemed to sense the strange heartbeat of the new world around him. He walked past the coconut peddlers where the men huddled around the carts loaded with coconuts sipping their rum mixed with the coconut milk. Some were on the third or fourth drink of the day. Some of the regulars smiled as he walked past. He had no time for them today.

Everywhere he looked he saw people. They were paired or in small groups. Talking, cackling, laughing out loud in public. And the hands going all the time. He watched the hands.

Looking for a weapon, for a menacing gesture. A slow moving car went by him and an attractive face smiled and winked. Then she saw his eyes and looked away.

He was beginning to get used to his new face. He was growing accustomed to its power.

He hailed a cab and got into the rear.

"Airport please." The long ride would take him to the outskirts of the capital.

You could spend a year in this strange country and not

come to really know its nature. The population is made up of the blacks that you find throughout the Caribbean, descendants of former slaves but what make Trinidad unique are the East Indian and Pakistani contingent of the population.

The blacks have a slight edge in the political arena, mostly sharing the power with the East Indians, but the latter, have the financial power. They are more educated and wealthier and run the country.

The poorer sections of the East Indian population are not like the rest of the Caribbean but more like India, prompting some of the most malicious and unfair comparisons to Calcutta and so they call Port of Spain the Calcutta of the Caribbean.

The taxi dropped him off in the main terminal and he made his way to the only lounge. He sat in the rear looking for privacy and a good vantage point. He nodded to a waitress and picked a corner table near the rear door leading to the bathrooms.

He ordered a Carib beer from the same waitress and sipped it as he looked at his watch. He was a little late, just enough time to be characteristically acceptable yet not so late as to insult his host but very early if you went by Trinidad time, where no one is on time, and an hour delay is the average.

From the corner of his eye he caught the movement towards the rear of the room and just barely moved his head to get a look at the two men who came in and began to speak. The younger of the two approached him slowly but deliberately with his hands in plain view. He wore a perfectly tailored "guayabera" starched stiff at   the collar.

The man was huge for a Cuban, six-foot-five at least, muscular thick body topped by a rugged face, his hair was light and curly that went well with his grey/blue eyes.

"Alex?", "I'm Manny."

They shook hands and sat down. Manny lit a cigarette and studied the young man facing him.

"First of all Alex I want to express my deepest sympathy over the loss of your father. He was an inspiration to us all."

He looked deeply into Alex's eyes.

Manny sensed the coldness and fear, but did not show it. Alex would not have noticed, except for Manny's casual glance at his bodyguard sitting at the counter making time with the waitress.

His mouth formed a softer smile and began to speak.

"When Martica Vega came to me I was surprised.

I have to tell you, I was skeptical at first. But she is very convincing. She is a true patriot and someone that I trust with my life, besides being one hell of a good looking woman." They shared a knowing look.

"I sensed that about her too, she is very intense when it comes to our struggle, and yes, she is a beautiful woman. My Father said she was someone that could be trusted, so we agree on both counts. She told me I had better be serious before talking to you, I convinced her, as I hope to convince you."

"OK, so now that we have that out of the way, you are probably wondering why you are here?"

As Manny spoke he glanced down every now and then. He used his index finger and traced what appeared to be the infinity symbol on the frosted moisture alongside the glass of beer as it stood in front of him. Alex lost his train of thought for a fraction of a second when he realized it was the numeral eight the older man was tracing.

Alex felt a bitter taste in his mouth. He could feel his face flush just slightly and the palms of his hands were moist. It was a sign that he was not yet in total control. But this was a moment that he had reflected about for so long, no time to vacillate or waver, for there would be no turning back. He averted Manny's eyes for a second and spoke calmly.

"I want to fight for my country". He looked him in the eyes.

Manny stubbed-out his cigarette on the ashtray and looked at Alex through narrowed eyes that signaled a change. The conversation was no longer about politics and polite chitchat.

"You know", he said, "I have a feeling that this has to do with your father's death."

Then Alex smiled a bit sardonically and began to speak the words that had been smoldering for so long.

"Yes, it has to do with my Father and Mother; I would be a fool to deny it. But this is about me. I've reached a turning point in my life. The road I have chosen is mine to take and I could sit here all night and try to explain it to you and you still wouldn't understand."

"I will never forget the   words of Zacarias Roldan, the so-called terrorist that was imprisoned for taking the fight to Fidel when you and I were just children. I visited him in jail once with my father when I was 19 and he looked straight at me and asked me what I was doing to fight for freedom. In my shameful silence I just looked at the frail man. He then told me he was setting bombs and burning cars at fifteen in the pursuit of freedom. Right then and there he judged me and all my generation basking in America's comfortable womb."

"I've been reborn. My Father and Mother's death was the catalyst, yes, but the new me is by choice. They were Cuba to me, now they are gone. I have lost the link with my past. Cuba is an alien country to me. I am not an American and I am not a Cuban.

I am a motherless and fatherless child. As I see it I have a choice to make. Become an American and continue my life as best as I can and move on. Or I can become a Cuban. To me a Cuban is either in Cuba or a patriot fighting to overthrow Castro. I have chosen to fight...to make Cuba proud of herself!"

A smile of understanding crossed Manny's face. They looked at each other once more, one final face-off, and shook hands.

"Come, then, welcome to the PRN (Partido Revolucionario Cubano-Cuban Revolutionary Party) we are going to strike a blow for freedom together." They walked together joined by the bodyguard and disappeared into the crowd.

Manny.

Before Manny became a terrorist, he was terrorized by life. When he was seven he had an argument with one of his cousins who in the heat of anger told him that his Mother was not the woman that raised him. He told him his real Mother was a whore that worked in El Oriente Café the most famous bordello in Santiago. This male cousin was two years older than him but it did not stop him from breaking his nose with a baseball bat. Strangely it was Manny that suffered the worst punishment. When he was older and wiser he began to realize that his cousin may have told him the truth. He searched through his parent's papers and found his birth certificates, two of them, the one his parents paid to have forged and the real one with the name of his real Mother and Father. He did not recognize the mothers name but his father's sent a chill up his spine.

His mother was a beautiful woman who could have become a wife and mother. But her fate was changed when her stepfather raped her and she ran away from home at the age of 17. She ended up living on the streets of Santiago where she was found by the woman who ran El Oriente Cafe. The madam a middle-aged woman who called herself Eva, and who had seen her better days decided to mold this pretty girl into the finest whore in her house. She became the favorite of the wealthy elite and the army officers. She was called "la Gallega" as she told everyone that she was born in Spain, to most Cubans all

Spaniards are called "Gallegos".

La Gallega wore old Spanish gowns and fanned her golden locks with expensive folding fans.

She was particularly fond of one Major who visited her once a month. He was a young officer from Camaguey who came to Santiago for his indiscretions. His name was Manuel Paz-Orta.

He treated her with kindness and showed her some affection. Whether by design or subconsciously, La Gallega stopped using protection when he made love to her. She became pregnant and hid the fact until she started showing a plump belly. The madam, a smart business woman, took her aside and counseled her to go to her family home for her confinement where they would take care of her until she gave birth on the condition that she return to the bordello afterwards. She had little choice, so she accepted.

She gave birth to a boy surrounded by strangers who cared for her but did not show any affection or sympathy for a woman who had suffered. Instead they persuaded her to leave the baby boy with them to be raised in a proper home and strongly suggested to her that she should go back to her life in Santiago. She pleaded for them to let her stay to raise the boy, but they told her she was to make her way on her own without any help nor support nor friendship from them. She took what little money she had and went off on her own. She landed in Caibarien on the coast and found a nice boarding home with a kind owner who helped take care of her and the baby. She doted on the boy and helped the old woman run the house and for a

few months she had a chance   at happiness. One of the
boarders, a fine looking young man from Cienfuegos who came
every few weeks for the boat races began to show interest in her.
They dated a few times and she acted as if her past did not exist.
She told him she was abandoned by her husband who went back
to Spain leaving her alone to face the world. She was for the first
time in her life a picture of motherhood.

The night he first kissed her was the night the famous
Hurricane hit the coastline after all reports had said it had turned
north and was dissipating. That night after she promised to
marry the good Arturo Darna, son of ranchers and graduate of
the university with a promising future, her fate was sealed for
good.

The storm not only made landfall at Caibarien, but with
winds in excess of 150mph. The boarding house was demolished
to the ground. During the worst of the storm the last thing she
heard was Arturo's voice calling out for her from downstairs as
she huddled with her baby inside an antique armoire made of
heavy oak that withstood the storm and the debris, and saved
both their lives. They were the only survivors along that whole
road that took the brunt of the storm.

She took it as an omen.

Facing the stark reality of making her way again without
any means nor friends nor family she gave up the baby to Eva's
family and went back to Santiago.

It took her almost a year to tell Manny's father he had a
son. He did not take it well. She assured him that he need not

worry about scandal nor gossip as the boy was being raised by a loving family as their own.

It would take seven years for his father to make General. But his ambitions were loftier than that. He betrayed his class and colleagues, he was one of the first upper level officers to join Castro's 26th of July Movement and quickly rose up the ranks in the Revolutionary Army. Castro never quite trusted him and assigned one of his most trusted boyhood friends, "the chameleon" as he was called, an intelligence expert, as Mannys father's adjutant and executive officer. His name was Alberto Menocal.

With the success of the revolution his father found himself in a position of power. He was given command of the army of the east and became the highest ranking official in that region. He ruled like a provincial governor from the old mayors offices in Santiago.

Once in complete control he began to tie up all his loose ends. La Gallega was lured at his persuasion to travel with him. She was handed airline tickets to Spain where she was taken to a house, drugged and smuggled to the Middle East and sold into slavery. She was never heard of again.

The young Manny whose given name was Pablo, waited until just the right time when he needed a friend the most to meet his father. He confronted him in his offices, the plush mayor's residence of Santiago. He struck a deal to keep his identity secret for a well paying job in his administration. He reluctantly agreed. His father the new General figured he could keep his eye on him.

The young Manny after many years of frustration over the failed economic policies of the administration, lost hope and made his escape from Cuba in a fishing boat. But before he left Cuba he married the daughter of Alberto Menocal (the chameleon), and quickly fathered a child. He left them behind under his care when he came to Miami.

Many years later when his father was tried for treason and drug trafficking and ended up in front of the firing squad, Manny had regretted his decision to leave, he wished he could have helped his father when he tried to save Cuba from Fidel and bring his country into the modern era without Soviet Communism.

He quickly joined the anti-revolutionary cause in exile in Miami, and took his dead fathers name of Manuel officially but not his now infamous last name. He went by his mother's maiden name of Suarez-Cuevas.

His father-in-law the chameleon accepted the fact that he had emigrated with regret but at the right time he made contact with his son-in-law and used him to gather information, he bribed him with money and supplied him with some information as well to keep him plugged in to the Castro regime and thereby created a double agent.

12

San Fernando, Trinidad and Tobago, 1998

It was early evening as they drove the unassuming Mazda compact through the narrow streets of San Fernando on the southern end of Trinidad. They traveled a short distance to the small suburb of Fyzabad. Here they picked up a tall very dark Muslim named Ayoub and he provided the final directions to find the small   house located in the middle of some Oil wells with their swinging arms harmoniously pumping the crude from the earth.

The house was the home of Trevor Bhagwan, a sympathetic Hindu and friend of Manny's and Mohan's.

They were warmly greeted and ushered inside.

"Come in, come in, my friends" Trevor greeted them with a thick Indian accent.

"Do you think we look suspicious, meeting you here in your home?" Manny said with half-squinted eyes of a person deep in serious thought.

A passerby turned his head ever so slightly without breaking his pace and continued down the road in front of the house.

What an ironic mix Alex thought, hindus and muslims working together. But such is the reality of the tropics.

"I used to visit one of my customers not far from here when I was a banker, and spent the night a couple of times. Trinidad is a quiet country without much violence; I believe coming here was a good choice." Alex said looking straight at their host who nodded in approval.

"Well let's get the show started; I don't want to take any chances." Manny added to end the debate.

After they all had settled the sleeping arrangements Alex, Trevor and Manny were the only ones that remained in the front porch of the home. From which they could see a small clearing just beyond the road and the oil field.

114

Alex was the last to join   them coming in at the end of
their discussion.

"Look, we've made all the arrangements, we spent a
month doing surveillance and we are ready from our end. The
next move is up to you. The decision to go with the mission is
yours, but I need to know by tomorrow or my contacts will
surely begin to ask questions." Trevor gestured to Alex to have a
drink.

They were drinking Chivas Regal with coconut water.
Alex took a sip and a memory of his grandfather, sipping his
coconut water with Gin made Alex think of the old man. He
quickly focused back on the men with him.

"Did you bring enough explosives to do the job?" Trevor
again seemed concerned.

"It better be enough, that's all I have to say, I didn't come
all the way down here to blow up a few palm trees, I want the
whole damn thing to blow." Manny winked at Alex.

"Well then we are ready and we start tomorrow at
sundown."

The Next Day at Dawn.

They were staring straight across from a small beach into
the surf when the sleek speed boat came in headed right for them
and the light Trevor was holding.

The 40ft "go fast" type hull was painted grey, like a
battleship. The driver signaled for them to wade out as he did

not want to get stuck in the   sand.

They made their way out to the boat and loaded all their heavy duffel bags and boxes. Then they climbed in through the stern diving ladder and greeted the captain, a rough looking Hindu who did not shake their hands nor greet them but told them to keep quiet and hang-on as he was going out fast.

Alex grinned at Manny and sat down in a rear bench seat just in front of the engine compartment. Manny sat in the chair next to the captain.

Alex heard the faint splash to his right, as he turned he saw a large tarpon or snook "crash" a school of mullet or pilchards, he could not tell which in the low light. It was exciting and wonderful; a memory of his grandfather fishing made him smile, but just as quickly faded. But he kept looking where the fish broke the surface. The big fish was full of strength and power. It was fear and survival for the bait fish. When the hungry predator broke the surface of the water it was forceful, precise, natural and beautiful. The bait fish were there. A meal. All huddled in the school, strength in numbers. They knew they would lose some, but there will always be more. An eerie strength in their plight. But there was a coveted strength in the sadness of their fate. They had faith. They had nothing but faith. We have everything and faith if we seek it. It just seems our faith is fleeting, coming and going with weekly reminders and rituals. Their faith is constant. Should it not be the same for us? There will always be more humans to replace the masses of armies.

The large groups who die for   their faith. There will always be more. How do they do it? Normal intelligent humans, sacrificed to do horrible things. The bait fish were there for food, the big fish was there to eat, and later he would be the food, the prey of bigger fish or man.

But Alex wondered if the fish's faith was stronger because of their numbers or their discipline. Probably both. He wondered if our faith would be stronger if we all had the same faith. Unite in one faith. That is all the prophets' words say. But each faith has their own prophets all saying the same. But it is just that unity in faith that makes man great and also weak. It makes them vulnerable to the predators that have no faith, just instincts and hunger. When you combine these two you get men and women who prey on the weak, Castro, Hitler and their kind throughout history.

Alex wondered if it would ever stop. No. Of course not. The danger is the weapons. Today is different. It could all end in a matter of minutes. He was afraid for his fellow man. Today he was Christian, a Muslim, a Hindu, and a Buddhist. We are one today. We are all in this one together. If there is a God he thought, he must show up soon! He was sure of this as he waited to begin a life of a predator. To strike at the weak in the name of freedom. He believed this totally and with conviction.

A Few Hours Later.

They were staring straight across from a beautiful 80 foot three-masted schooner with the name La Palma. What an incongruity, but then the entire harbor full of oil tankers and other ships slept incongruously in the calm waters of the Orinoco basin. Such a lovely harbor in a warm tropical setting.

"Do you think we look suspicious? There's an awful lot of big ships out there, but not one speedboat?" It was Manny who spoke, gingerly pulling the rocket launchers out of the bags and cases.

"Look all we have to do is find our target and get on with our special delivery. Just be on the lookout for patrol boats." Manny said nonchalantly as he assembled the hand-held rockets.

"There...the big one over there, there she is the Russian Tanker *Workers Paradise*." Trevor walked back from the bow pointing to the ship still wearing the night vision goggles.

"All right lets get close captain, and be ready to get out fast." Manny ordered.

The big man nodded his head in acknowledgment.

Manny, Alex, and Trevor hoisted the compact Russian made RPG-18 rocket propelled grenade launchers on their shoulders.

"You have your targets, right?" Manny asked one last time.

"Yes!" Trevor replied.

Alex just nodded.

When they were no more than 150 meters from the ship's side the speedboat turned broadside to the tanker.

"OK, One two three!" It was Manny who fired first after his command aiming at the base of the smokestack. Then Alex followed with Trevor whose rockets were aimed near the waterline just aft of the fourth bulkhead.

The sound of the explosions was ear-shattering. The H.E.A.T. (High Explosive Anti Tank) warheads they were using could penetrate up to 375 millimeters of steel. The fuse of the heat rounds detonated on impact. The captain gunned the engines of the speedboat and they were speeding out of the harbor as the secondary explosions, heaved a mountain of fire into the dark night. They had hoped to ignite the oil and destroy the ship completely. They had not counted on the cargo of munitions and arms that were stowed in the hidden cargo compartments bought in the black market of Macao.

They were almost a mile away when they heard the last roaring blast send a huge tower of fire and smoke and watched as the three-masted schooner caught fire from the flying debris that spread for almost a quarter mile from the now blazing tanker.

"Coño!" was all that Manny could say as he patted Alex on the back.

"Viva Cuba Libre!" he replied. But he looked back sadly and watched the schooner burn to the waterline, sink and disappear.

A Few Days Later.

Back in the Port of Spain Airport awaiting their flight out of Trinidad Manny took Alex aside and told him where to meet for the next assignment.

"You're going to get a kick out of this one," he began with a wicked grin, "we've got this new gal who Valentin is seeing that used to work in Disney World, she used to play one of the characters, Snow White and sometimes subbed for Minnie Mouse. Anyhow she gets fired and returns to Miami and tells Valentin that she knows her way around the underground tunnels like the back of her hand. So you know Val, he charms the pants off her until she is crazy about him and he convinces her to join the party. So now we go and get her to tell us everything with Alberto taking notes in his laptop and we have the specs and blueprints of the whole fucking place. So we took a vote and we are going to blow up the Castle. The fucking Disney Castle at peak hour." He stopped himself to laugh.

"I can't believe it, the heart of the American heartstrings, Mickey Mouse's house. Brilliant, just *friggin* brilliant." Alex joined in the laughter.

But deep in his soul something shook, something that had been plaguing him for while. Why would Cubans want to blow-up Disney World? How is that a blow to Castro?

The seeds of his new life were sprouting a bitter harvest.

13

Miami Beach, Florida 1999

Miami Beach, where the dejected, restless souls of our senior citizens used to come and drift through their golden years was different now.

They all came now, not just the old Jews.

The old worked hard all their lives to save enough money to come to Miami Beach. And in the strip of beach nestled among the new Ocean Drive they dreamed of spending their last years "fighting against the dying of   the light" as Dylan Thomas so eloquently wrote, in warmth and comfort. But the new wave of Hispanics, and the yuppies hungry for ocean views and nightlife had transformed the fountain of youth that was South Beach to a trendy hotspot with few equals. The elderly Jews that could moved north to Normandy Isles or to Central Florida.

Gone are the cheap hotels and motels where the old and poor could live on cheap rent just a few blocks from the beach. The very same Hotels and Motels have become trendy, posh "boutique" mini-resorts. Most offering great nightlife and restaurants rivaling New York and Paris. And music, every conceivable taste is satisfied. But the trendy tend to make the glitzy clubs where the stars come to mingle with the masses the focal point of the new Miami Beach.

The Miami Beach Convention Center sits in the middle of a nest of those revamped new condos and apartment houses.

The city spent quite a few dollars for their center. But it was worth every penny! The Beach is a natural for conventions. Year after year the salesmen, managers, dealers, Republicans and Democrats. They all came. Where better to hold a large gathering of the pesso-novantes but the land of endless sunshine and salsa? Take a dip in the ocean, hire an exotic escort and enjoy the fruits of your labor.

And of course don't forget your greenbacks. Yes'sir we sure love those damn Yankees and their good old money.

The AFL-CIO National convention was coming to a close tonight. And it was ending in style. The honorable Lindsay Birch

Jameson, the first female president of the United States of America would speak at the closing ceremonies.

The Ultra Liberal president was trying to strengthen her good relations with the unions. It was expected that she would announce the details of the new labor bill.

Not all the union rank and file agreed with nor supported her, but collectively as a group she needed them. She would be well-received.

By 6:00PM a large crowd had gathered in the parking lot. They awaited the arrival of the President. It was common knowledge that she would arrive around that time.
A large area was completely cordoned by police and plainclothes secret service agents.

Just to the left of the crowd towards the rear, a heavily guarded group of demonstrators shouted and chanted.

The placards and signs carried the same slogans.
"Better Dead than Red"
"Free Cuba Now"
"Lindsay and Fidel, lovers and partners in Crime"

They numbered in the thousands and would not be restrained in their fervor. They hated the liberal President and all that she stood for.

The new President would be lifting the embargo soon as they expected her to do. But in the campaign she side-stepped the question like a good politician.

The normal crowd of well-wishers and proud citizens in the front moved about uneasily awaiting the arrival of the

President. Every now and then some of them would look over their shoulder at the demonstrators behind them and fidget uncomfortably. Such an embarrassment for them and their president to be so humiliated.

There was a long stretch of quiet as the crowds strained to hear the advancing distinct sounds of helicopters.

Everyone strained with anticipation.

A loud roar went up as they slowly passed over them and hovered over the crowds for some time and then flew around the convention center and headed south towards the city.

It would not be until an hour later that an announcement was made that the president's visit was cancelled due to illness.

Everyone was overcome with disappointment.

A block away on the top floor apartment of a penthouse overlooking the convention and the throngs of people. Manny cursed loudly in front of Alex and Henry.

"Hijo de puta!!!" (Son of a bitch!!!)

"Que carajo paso!!!" (What the fuck happened!!!)

"It's over let's get the hell out of here in case our cover is broken." Manny said to Alex.

"Si, Si, vamonos".

"Henry, get your stuff and let's get out of here."

The young man they called Henry, who the hell knew what his real name was, began to dismantle his sniper's rifle and gently placed the parts into the case that resembled a saxophone.

When he was finished he said.

"I want the rest of my   money now, if you don't mind."

Manny thought for a moment and looked at Alex who looked back with that, please don't start something look.

"Sure, it's not your fault. But since you did not complete the mission can we ask for a discount?"

Alex could only smile at his friend. Such "cojones"! (Balls)

Here they were standing in front of one of the worlds deadliest assassins and he is trying to cut a deal! God bless him! Crazy bastard.

Henry looked amused but he smiled and said. "Sure, take 10% off the balance."

Manny reached into his bag and removed $500K from the bag and handed him the bag containing the balance of $4.5 Million less the discount.

They all scurried into their cars and disappeared in seconds.

The Night Before.

The night before the assassination was to take place Alex sat in his favorite restaurant on South Beach, IL' POSTINO named after the movie and located in the Sea Lust Hotel on Ocean Drive. He sat with a young Venezuelan girl that he had paid for from the man that he had met at the restaurant the night before. He had befriended him at the bar. After some high priced single-malts the man said he   could provide him with some company for the night. It was the alcohol that worked on his resolve. And when he introduced the young woman, Alex was helpless. He would act impulsively, again. He spent the night making love, correction, fucking her brains out.

In the morning he heard himself smile and shook his head at his reflection in the mirror.

"Hey lover'" she said seductively, "I had a wonderful time last night, why don't we spend the day together, no money, just you and me. We can go to the beach, hang out here and have more fun, later we can go to dinner or a movie…"

"Teresita, my precious, I have to work today, so I can't, as much as it hurt me to say it we shall have to say goodbye, but give me your number and I will call you when I'm next in town."

"You sure, you want to leave me like this?" She uncovered herself to him.

"I'm afraid I must. But here is another $500 for you to go shopping and have some fun on your own."

He walked her down to the street holding her hand as if they were old friends and lovers and put her in a taxi.

Then he walked down the beach and when he reached a secluded payphone, he called Mark.

He held the receiver for few minutes reflecting on what he would say; it had been almost two years since he had spoken to his father in law. He knew his ruse of insinuating his suicide would not convince Mark, he would know he didn't have the balls to kill himself.

"Hello Mark, its me…"

"I knew you'd call someday, I've been praying for you son. Are you all right?"

"Yes, Mark I don't want to waste any more of your time that I have to, I also don't want to talk about me, is Linda all right?"

"You know her, she has moved on, she has made a new life for herself, she's a tough 'old bird."

"I'm glad, Mark I'm going to tell you something that is going to sound crazy, I want no questions or explanations, If the president appears tonight for her speech she will be assassinated, I will not give you anything more than the Presidents life. I do this for you and Linda and whatever conscience I have left. If you do not believe me it will be on your shoulders".

"Alex we know that you are involved with the PRC, my son come in, I can help, you are too smart and good for these people, please…"

"Mark, I have to go, you take care now, forget about me."

He hung up the phone and hailed a taxi. He sat in the rear seat thinking of her. The last time he saw her was when he had followed her to the campus, he had watched her from a distance as she got out of her father's car and ran to her classes. He felt he could almost touch her when he traced her steps to smell the perfume trail she left behind.

14

Cuban coastline near Cojimar, 1999

There is a fishing boat in the distance. It looks like a homemade "Cienfuguero" type. An open hull made of wood planking about eighteen to twenty feet in length, with a small engine in the center. There appears to be two fishermen, but it's too far to tell, there may be more. It seems to stand still, but it could also be doing a   slow troll, or drift fishing. But at this depth they would not be anchored. Alex wondered what they were after. Tuna and swordfish most likely.

It would be quite a battle if they hooked a big marlin. He thought of The Old Man and the Sea. And then realized that they must be very close to Cojimar, where Hemingway based his timeless story.

Funny how he had been reading the very same book just a month ago when he found an old copy amongst his books. He was feeling much better after a short bout of flu and the book had helped him pass the usual down-time that accompanies the malady.

The day was just breaking and the sun began its rise on the horizon creating that shimmering golden highway on the sea. Some gulls are skimming over the surface, every now and then stopping to rest in the water. Alex thought about a shark coming from underneath and gobbling it up in one great big bite. He smiled and felt the early morning breeze on his face and watched the incandescent ball rise slowly in the horizon. He wondered if it was his time to rise up and seize the day. The sea was speaking to him this morning.

The island of Cuba was trying to hide under a blanket of clouds. A thin row of wispy clouds that seemed to move ever so slowly revealing green hills, and the unmistakable outline of paradise.

Manny was driving the catamaran speedboat with Orlando beside him. They seemed at ease, as if on a joyride to

Bimini and not to a dangerous   place armed to the teeth with an army that hated what they stood for, he sensed they must have made this run before. There was no worry that they would also be visible to the fishing boat or any coast guard vessel that would be patrolling the waters.

Alex looked away from the shore and back over the stern to where they had come from. It seemed like just an hour had gone by and not the real three hours from Marathon. He began to think about the night before in bed with Martica. She had been especially artful in her lovemaking, exhausting him to the point of his begging her to stop and let him catch some sleep before embarking on this adventure. She had briefed him earlier about a secret mission that Manny wanted him to be part of.

Some adventure, infiltrating back to his homeland. Sneaking in and out of Cuba on some secret mission that Manny would not divulge.

The speedboat had finally slowed down. Alex joined them at the helm.

"That looks like an inlet over there". Alex said pointing to a clump of mangroves.

To anyone who does not know the shallow waters in most Caribbean coastlines they would not realize that the mangroves can be like small islands with inlets or navigable canals surrounding them. Some are manmade to allow access to dry land; others like this particular one were natural. The only problem was knowing the depth of the water. Without sufficient clearance they could run aground. Alex figured they needed about two and half to three feet for this boat.

"Yep, that's where we   go in and work our way to dry land. I just hope we have enough water. We had to come in at this time and not at night to catch the highest tide. Manny said as he made his way slowly into the inlet.

"I just hope that fishing boat we passed a while back doesn't turn us in." Alex said nonchalantly.

"Don't worry about it".

He navigated the boat with knowledge. Alex was now sure he'd done it before.

They made their way slowly turning frequently to stay in the middle of the channel. The air became thick and moist with humidity. The mangroves impeded whatever breeze was blowing adding to their discomfort.

The next turn they made did not make sense to Alex, he had seen Orlando pointing to a small tributary of the main channel barely wide enough for the boat to navigate. Manny relinquished control of the helm to the younger man who made a beeline for the small opening. He drove about two hundred meters and turned into another small channel that traveled for about fifty meters before opening into a small lagoon surrounded by thick mangroves on every side. The lagoon was barely wide enough for the 35 foot boat. Orlando maneuvered the boat perfectly around the lagoon and brought the bow facing the entrance they had just come through. He pushed a button and the anchor dropped from the bow pulpit. The engines stopped and they floated quietly like a cork that falls into the wine bottle sometimes, slowly turning with the current.

Manny shook Orlando's hand. "Great job, now when is the next high tide at night?" he asked him.

"Seven thirty tonight".

"Perfect, we will leave then."

"What happens now?" Asked Alex

"We wait."

A half-hour passed before the three of them turned to the channel entrance and watched as the small fishing boat that they had seen earlier made its way into the lagoon and pulled up next to them.

They had their hands on their pistols watching every move the two men and a woman made.

"Como estas Manolito", the woman spoke first.

"Coño Melina, I didn't recognize you." He relaxed and pulled the woman onboard kissing her on the cheek and hugging her warmly.

"It's my new hair, thanks to the tint you brought me last time you were here. You like?" She posed coquettishly.

"I do," said Orlando first, hugging her tightly to him and kissing her cheek, "Estas bellisima, Meli".

"Gracias mi negro bello". She held his face in both of hers and kissed him back on both cheeks.

She looked at Alex.

"And this must be the new patriot we have heard so much about". She came to him and reached out with delicate hand.

"Melina Novo".

"Alejandro." He said taking stock of the engaging eyes on a naturally beautiful face without any make-up, surrounded by billowing locks of red hair barely restrained in a thick pony tail.

"Ay, "dios mio", a cuban man of few words. How refreshing." She flirted with him.

"Vamonos, we don't have time for chit chat, we need to be back by seven latest to catch the tide." With this final order Manny led them into the smaller boat and they made their way back to the main channel and headed for the mainland.

It was then Alex had the premonition that his father was with him. He could almost hear him, *"look out for those that seem to know everything, they are dangerous because of their ignorance"*, he used to tell him. Now for the first time since starting this crazy adventure he worried. But in his fear he also felt a proud, almost surreal feeling of being home. After all this was the land of his father, his beloved grandfather and his precious mother who cut her wrists and left him alone. And now here he was coming home. But he was right when he said it before; Cuba was an alien country to him.

They arrived at modern dock that stretched out about fifty meters from the rear of a plantation style home hidden by mangroves around the edge of the water and coconut palms and sea grape trees in the yard in front of the house. Along the entire length of the house ran a verandah with some comfortable chairs and rockers and to one side a very inviting hammock.

As soon as they had docked and Orlando tied the last of

the mooring ropes, a group of   two women and man wearing a military uniform came from the house. The two women ran to the visitors, and Alex could see one of them was no more that 12 or 13, the other was older perhaps 60, they both went straight for Manny who took them into his arms and kissed and hugged them both. The soldier stayed in the verandah waiving to them to come in.

The group then began to greet warmly, all except Alex who watched.

"Alex, this is my wife Marina and my daughter Estrella, and over on the verandah is my father-in-law, Colonel Alberto Menocal." *The chameleon himself.*

Alex shook hands with his wife and Estrella came to him and kissed him on the cheek. My name is Star in English. She told him proudly in her best English.

"It's beautiful, like you." He told her.

She said thank you and grabbed his arm and escorted him to the house.

The Colonel came over to Alex and said that he had known his father. They had been at the University together. He always liked and admired him. It was then that Alex recognized the medical insignia. He was not regular army.

"You know I remember one time when your father was leading a student demonstration and we were all shouting and creating a big disturbance at the administration building of the University when your father went up to the front and climbed on top of one of the statues and began to scream obscenities at the military that had come in to   shut us down. When they tried to get him down we all rallied to him and the military backed away. Later he went into hiding right here in my family home for a couple of months until the furor died down. My father and mother were very fond of him. I miss them terribly, they were older and have since gone to our savior."

At this last statement Alex was confused, here was a man in uniform a member of the worst totalitarian regime whose army ruled with an iron fist over his people, and he was talking about his father and faith in God.

The older wiser man looked Alex in the eyes.

"In Cuba what you see most times is not what it seems, we are a country of shadows and broken pieces of glass, every piece a secret, we lead many lives in order to survive."

It was eerie that this man who had known his father and probably his mother would invoke the very last words of his mother. He immediately felt an uneasy connection.

A Few Hours Later.

Sometimes without conscious realizations, our thoughts, our faith, even our beliefs are filtered through our past. We talk about other times, other places, other persons and lose touch with our present. Sometimes we think if we could just go back in time we would be happy. But anyone who attempts to reenter the past is sure to be disappointed. Anyone who has ever visited the place of his birth after years of absence is shocked by the differences between the way the place   actually is, and the way he remembered it. He may walk along old familiar streets and roads, but he is a stranger in a strange land. He has thought of the place as home, but he finds he is no longer here, even in spirit. He has gone on to a new and different life, and in thinking strongly of the past, he has been giving thought and interest to something that no longer really exists.

Alex stood in front of his boyhood home in Jaimanitas, Cuba and try as he might he could not connect. He stood and tried to remember the front porch where he had kissed the little girl neighbor that was dressed in her mother's clothing who sang songs to him and came up to his face and with lipstick stained lips planted a kiss on his lips.

He remembered he wiped the waxy stickiness off with his arm and called her an ugly name. Then he watched her break into adolescent tears and run away crying to her mother.

That memory clung to his brain cage, but nothing else. The house was dingy, overgrown with ugly trees and wild grass. The roof edges showed rust encrusted iron bars, as the cement had broken off at intervals. There was also an addition to the carport. A whole new apartment had been fashioned. As he stood there he could not connect with his past. This small unassuming rabble of a house could not have been the one he remembered so new so big and spacious.

"Bueno, have you seen enough, are you sufficiently depressed, now?" Manny was saying to him.

"What, ah…yes, let's get out of here. There is nothing but

confusion here, I've seen   enough of my past. I don't really know this place anymore."

If we cannot connect with our past on the physical level, how can we even begin to explain our connection with our spiritual self? Why do we feel the way we do about our childhood memories of home after many years away? We are a sentimental lot.

Alex thought to himself as he looked at a neighborhood that could not be the one he remembered. He was indeed a stranger in his hometown.

There was a pain in the back of Alex's head, a headache that he did not experience very often.

It was the same headache he felt for weeks after his parents died. The low-grade pain moving in small electrical impulses from the top of his neck and up the back of his brain. He knew the only way to get rid of it was to think of something he loved, like fishing, sex, or at last resort a good buzz from two double Scotch whiskeys.

"No chance to stop for drink somewhere?" He said out loud.

"No way, this little excursion is bad enough we don't want to take any unnecessary chances." The Old Colonel sitting in the passenger side reached into the glove compartment and produced a flask and held it out to Alex.

He took it and drank, the smooth peaty taste of good single malt scotch whiskey made its way painfully down his throat but within minutes his pain left replaced with that familiar shrouding buzz.

They drove another hour before they stopped on a side road

just far enough from the main   road not to be seen, to eat some sandwiches Manny's wife had prepared. They ate quickly washing down the food with *"café con leche"* that the Colonel poured out of an old thermos into some paper cups for each of them.

They arrived at the house around three in the afternoon. They parked across the street and watched for several minutes. A black woman dressed in a white uniform came out of the house andwalked away in the opposite direction. The colonel put his hand up.

"Let's give her a few seconds…Ok lets go."

They got out of the car and walked quickly and through the wrought iron gate and up the short walkway and stood in the porch of the house. Manny was looking through the window panes as the Colonel worked on the old fashioned door handle and entry lock. With a loud click the door slowly opened groaning softly and they made their way inside.

The Colonel led the way.

They walked slowly and quietly, but the hard marble floors would not betray them. Marble is hard and cold. They could have jumped up and down and the floor would not make a sound. The Colonel made his way into the study where he went directly to a small closet in one corner of the room, and on the floor was a small carpet. He lifted the carpet from one edge and revealed a floor safe. He worked the tumblers knowingly and the safe opened. He reached inside and pulled out some stacks of dollar bills, which he gently put to one side. Then he pulled out a letter sized envelope that was about a half-inch thick. It was not sealed. He opened the flap and removed the folded   papers.

It appeared to be some sort of dialogue between two characters. Alex tried to read but was gently nudged by Manny who had a small camera in his hand. He was making room on the floor and the colonel began to position the pages in groups of four in a square and Manny began to take two pictures of each set. It took them no more than a two or three minutes to photograph all the pages and then the Colonel put them back in the envelope and replaced it in the safe, along with the cash.

Manny gave Alex a wink, with a grin. Alex shrugged.

Before leaving the house the Colonel went into one of the rooms. Inside was a large bed with an old man sleeping in the center of the bed. He looked tired and his skin was pale. The Colonel went to the nightstand that was covered with medicine bottles and picked several up to read the labels before he picked one out and replaced it with one he had in his pocket.

He looked back at the other two men and gave them a "thumbs up". He walked back and joined them. They made their way out of the house and looking over the street, walked back to their car.

"What did you give him?" Manny asked as he drove on the road back.

"A little Valium cocktail, he will sleep peacefully for a couple of hours. I wasn't worried about him; I was worried the nurse on the next shift would be on time. But I gave her a special assignment to delay her for fifteen minutes. I think I saw her coming when we drove away. It was perfect timing. I think we pulled it off."

"What's in the papers?" Alex asked.

"I'll tell you when we get back to America." Was all his friend offered.

Alexander

"Ye shall know the truth, and the truth shall make you free."

-Jesus Christ (John 8:32)

15

Miami Florida three weeks later.

Death should not be premeditated it should be as a semi-envious, anticipatory, expectant farewell...something like..."*Oh, you're leaving now...how natural for you at this time. I WILL see you again. You will be missed here. I know, but I'm glad to go now. Love is forever, never forget that.*"

Just that low-key sort of thing. No huge angst. A certain all pervasive peace that comes from the certain knowledge that; **1.** Death is inevitable and **2.** That it is a natural transition, not a final tragedy, more like an adventure.

Alex liked that. It sounded very good to him. He'd always thought that death would be a new adventure.

To the atheist he was, it was pure rationalization, for the truth was that he feared death and the stench of death was all over him.

It was a strange world that Alex entered on this his 35th birthday. No romantic ties, no immediate plans. The only direction was that of the "la causa" (the cause) and that was to him the cloudiest of all ideals. He didn't really know what it was; to him it meant doing something to avenge his father, to come to grips with the glorious memory of his grandfather and his "patria" (fatherland). He only knew that he was deeply involved now.

Was it self-destruction? Or self-pity? Or perhaps the startling realization that his very existence on this planet so far amounted to absolutely nothing. All his life he had dreamed of glory. But it was elusive.

These thoughts weighed heavily on his mind as he heard the knock on the door.

No one could possibly know that he was here. *A moment of panic.* He went to the door with his Glock.

Before he could say anything the voice came through from the other side in harsh whisper.

"Alex! Open-up it's me." The voice was strained, but it was his friend.

Alex opened the door and Manny almost fell on him. He was holding his abdomen and looked pale and in pain.

"What the hell happened to you?"

"We've been betrayed,   I barely made it, and I don't know if we're safe here. They are all dead!" Manny grimaced in pain as Alex laid him on the couch.

"Who's dead?" He repeated. "Who's dead?"

"Martica, Valentin, Edgar, Menacho… all of them…dead."

Manny spoke softly but clearly, every name evoking a memory.

"As soon as I rest we must go. Call Orlando in Marathon, tell him he has to get us out of the country in his boat."

"Sure…sure, but rest now and I'll call him."

"Use a pay phone, I don't know what they have, your phone may be tapped."

"Will you be all right while I go? Can I get you anything?"

"I'm good now, I think the bleeding has stopped, Valentin threw himself in the path of the bullets or I...I just need to rest for a minute." He said drifting into a semi sleep.

"You rest and I will be right back."

The room was fast becoming a very small cell, a cell of fear and tension. And now like a cell it was about to divide. Yes, just like a living cell divides. We go back as individual cells. Disperse, re-assemble, our body's a box, thus the magnetic attraction to Love, Hate etc. Cells want to reintegrate in previous incarnations, if that is your thing.

Alex's face was dripping sweat, his heart and pulse raced.

He walked out of the room and felt better instantly. But he walked hurriedly to the pay phone in the lobby.

"Mark, it's me again."   There was short pause.

"I've been expecting, hoping that you called, are you all right?"

"So far, but the PRC has been hit hard... lot's of bodies. What can you tell me?"

"Not much, but you need to get out of the country now!"

"Anywhere I should avoid?"

"Trinidad, Venezuela and Mexico and Central America, Go as far south as you can, and disappear."

"Anything else?"

"I can't, I've already stuck my neck out as far as I dare. Go right now and don't look back. I have to go. God be with you. And Alex, we did not do this; this operation was bred in Havana!"

"Thanks, when I feel safe we need to talk."

Alex dialed Orlando and told him to get the boat ready to go in an hour with enough fuel for a long haul.

Before going upstairs he drove his car around the rear of the safe house and exchanged plates with a pick-up truck safely parked in resident parking spot of the next apartment building.

He helped Manny into the passenger seat and drove away towards US 1 heading south.

By the time they got to the eighteen mile stretch between Florida City and the mainland to Key Largo, Alex's mood was noticeably lighter as they started to leave the cities and the rush behind, his fear had unleashed out into the mangroves that surrounded them and he felt   peace again. It would not last. Towards the end after the second passing lane, Manny awoke from his sleep. His face was paler and his lips purple, his eyes listless. Alex feared he would not make it to Marathon.

His lips moved and formed words.

"I have sinned all my life, in the name of freedom; I have figured it all out now…now I can bare the truth…"

His face looked ahead, as if Alex was not next to him.

"Your father was getting too close to the truth…"

Manny's body was almost lifeless now. He just stared ahead, but his eyes were vacant now. Nothing in there. His body a cage of pain and his eyes trapped inside. So communicative, spoke volumes…so eloquent. He was dying.

"I ask you to tell my family that I love them; they are the only good in my life."

The body is indeed a shell; the eyes giant reflectors that mirror collective cells merging their electrical impulses into that bright light. Cells die. Light goes out. Body is a shell, a cage. Like snails we are. Carrying around all our baggage in our "house".

Alex looked at him trying to understand his last words about his father, he thought Manny was delusional. On the seat a pool of blood was soaking into the upholstery growing in diameter and dripping unto the floor of the car. A thin trickle of blood made its way down from the left corner of his mouth, his blank eyes blinked and flickered for a moment as he struggled to breathe.

"I ask God for forgiveness for all my sins, I have killed men, women and children and I am sorry for all I've done. But you my friend must forgive me for my greatest sin..."

"Manny my friend I forgive you, please rest..."

"You are not my friend and soon you will know that I'm not yours either... I know it was you who betrayed us at Disney."

"You're delusional..." Alex said unable to look the dying man in the eyes.

"It was you who diffused the bomb in the Castle. You went back to pick-up your bag of explosives; I followed you and saw you coming out of the basement. At that time I did not think you capable of betraying us. But after the fiasco with the President we all figured we had a mole in the organization, it was you who saved the President's life."

"Manny..."

"Let me finish, I don't have much time. When I started to investigate I put it together. I knew it was you. But I didn't say anything. I know you did it for some pathetic spiritual reason; you are not working for the American bastards who betrayed us and sold us out to the Russians. No, you did it for something else. I was close to finding out, it doesn't matter now, it's all finished. But I held back my thoughts because I owed you. Here are the documents we brought from Cuba, they are my father's last-will and testament, they will prove that he was innocent of all the trumped up charges against him when they shot him.

There are names, dates   and facts that will help bring down the Castro brothers. They must get to the right people, people who will make sure it exposes the truth"

"You don't owe me shit and I don't want the responsibility, what I want is out of this nightmare."

"Alex, forgive me, you will know the truth soon enough."

"There's nothing to forgive."

"No, YOU must forgive me...I...I...killed your father."

With his last breath Manny's words seared and cut into his flesh. Probing like a scalpel engraving madly a living reminder on his soul.

He did all he could to keep the car on the road for the next few miles. For he could not look away from the death mask on the face of his friend whose lifeless eyes judged him from the other side, the dark side.

And if a fellow traveler could hear beyond the rolled-up windows as they drove by, they would hear the sobs and tears of a man in anguish who had at last reached the doors of Hades and was poised to enter into eternal damnation.

17

The Florida Straits, Gulf of Mexico two hours later.

Orlando Cortina shook with fright. "I hate to be near a dead body, it gives me the creeps." He said shaking his dreadlocks in disgust.

"I used to fear the dead too, you could not get me near a cemetery when I was a boy, then one day my mother told me that I should fear the living and not the dead for they can't hurt you anymore." Somehow Alex did not truly believe her right now. For as he wrapped Manny's body in the canvas tarp and tightly tied rope all around the body he felt that this lifeless body of his friend/tormentor was still gnawing at his gut.

They tied the largest anchor they had to the bundle and dropped him over the gunwale of the boat. The depth finder showed that they were in 1600 feet of water. Somewhere over the Florida Straits

Orlando looked at Alex as if waiting for him to say something.

"We commend this body to the Ocean we ask that you accept his soul into your kingdom and forgive his many sins which he repented with his final words. And I ask for the wisdom and strength to forgive him for his sin against me, for I don't know if I can ever forgive him."

"Amen." Said the big black man next to him giving him a puzzled look but he did not question him and he did not say anything else.

Orlando gunned the engines and the boat sped away into the dark.

"I'm going to try to get some sleep, wake me if you get tired, Ok." Alex said to his friend. Orlando nodded.

In the cramped cabin he tried to make himself comfortable in the V-berth. Once he was settled he could see out of the porthole and to the sky and stars. He felt cold; the army blanket that smelled of dried fish was rough on his skin and did not warm him. He rolled away from the porthole and hugged two lifejackets and used another as a pillow. The words of his dead friend rang in his ears. He opened and closed his eyes and looked about the tight space.

The resentment began to build slowly, he tried to understand, but he could not. All he felt was anger. At himself, at his dead friend at God and at his mother for leaving him alone to grief. He wasn't prepared for the tears. When he felt them build up in his eyes, he shut them and fought them back. They receded once more into that dark place. When he felt drowsy, he rubbed his eyes and heard his voice. "God Help Me." He kept repeating, a pleading… a prayer from a place he did not know, at least that is what he thought. Then surrendering to exhaustion he let go. He finally slept soundly with the sea rocking him like a cradle.

At dawn he awoke and came out of the cabin of the Magnum Catamaran. They had made very good time and Orlando pointed to the distant horizon.

"The Yucatan is there we should be in Cabo Catoche within a couple of hours and then to Progreso before Noon. If you take the helm I can catch a quick power nap before we get there." And he went inside and was asleep in seconds.

Alex held the wheel checked the heading on the compass and watched the sea glide by. He loved watching the sun rise even though he hardly ever did it. And he loved the clouds as they played with the fading Moon and let her peek out from above, from below, from the side, some were grey or in the distant some were black and up above near the sun and moon they were blue or pink or any shade in between to match the color of the rising sun and the setting moon.

He gazed at the ocean   all the way to the horizon and wondered about what awaited him.

Alex reached into the leather duffel bag that he had quickly packed with all his belongings and reached for the money belt he had found on Manny's body when he dressed him for his burial. He counted out $130,000 in cash. But the cash was not what caught his eye, it was the worn envelope about half and inch thick that accompanied the cash, he recognized it immediately.

It took him all of an hour to read the whole transcript.

Orlando came out of the cabin after a while and stretched and pointed to the horizon.

"Mexico lindo!" he said as he pointed.

Just east of Progreso they put in at a makeshift dock barely wide enough for a man to walk. It just lead to a beach where you had to walk for a quarter mile to a small fishing Village. Orlando said he had picked up a group of Cuban exiles here a few years back.

In the ramshackle cantina where he and Orlando drew some stares Alex found a phone. He overpaid in dollars for the use of the phone and called Mark.

"It's me."

"Where are you son?"

There was no hesitation he had no one else to turn to.

"Mexico near Merida."

He would put his life in the hands of his father-in-law once again.

"I think you should go   south into Ecuador and then Peru or Colombia. I can help smuggle you with my contacts. Give me an hour and call me back, I will make some calls. You will need cash."

"Ok, thanks." He hung up.

The locals warmed up to them and their dollars and offered cold Coronas and Dos XX's which they gladly took and when they brought them tacos and tortillas filled with some kind of spicy meat they ate hungrily. He had forgotten his hunger. It made the overly spicy food go down easier.

"I need to get going fast, I have to top-off my tanks in Progresso at a friend's Marina and get going again, he might have something for me to take back, see if I can make some money on this trip." Orlando spoke chewing his taco.

"My brother don't take any unnecessary chances don't stop anywhere or talk to anyone get out fast and get home safely, here take this envelope it has $20,000 in cash I will not see you for a long time. I can't emphasize enough to stay low for at least a year and avoid people, even if they say they are PRC, trust no one."

Orlando looked at him sadly.

"There is an envelope inside with the cash. Do not open it until you get to Marathon. Inside you will find a letter addressed to you with instructions to call a man named Mark and his number. My instructions are clear; tell him exactly what I've written down in the letter and hang up. You are going to have to trust me and him. Do whatever he tells you. I owe you my life, my brother, take care of yourself and forget me. I do not exist."

They hugged. "Coño, I'm going to miss you my brother." The black man said finally releasing him.

He made the young man promise on his mother's soul. For he knew him to be brash and liked to gamble and live the good life. But he liked his black friend; he was a fisherman like his grandfather and had taken him out many times in his "other" boat, the one he chartered out of Grassy Key. A great cover for a smuggler dashing around the warm tropical waters of the Caribbean.

They embraced again. And the younger man told him before he left.

"Go with God brother."

That would leave Alex with around $110,000 in cash that he carried in Manny's belt around his waist. He was confident that with a little luck he could hide in the mountains for long time.

As he waited for his call he sat by the waters edge sipping from a bottle of Dos XX and his thoughts again turned to Manny and the first time he met him. How he had told him how much he admired and respected his father.

He always felt that the Cuban militant refugees never trusted his father and his diplomacy towards a peaceful resolution to the struggle for Freedom.

But to carry the secrets that this man, this terrorist, traitor, patriot, carried with him as he became his friend and mentor was the supreme lesson he could have learned. The players in this game were coldhearted killers; he knew he was not like them. But at present the only choice was to keep one step ahead of them and stay alive. For he now possessed information that could shake the foundations of power in the Western Hemisphere, it was not what he wanted. He looked forward to losing himself. To going somewhere where there were no politics or guns, to find sanctuary in this violent world. Considering the events of the last 24 hours he was thinking he might be overly optimistic.

18

Merida, Mexico six hours later.

Alex read the short note that he had scribbled quickly about the Coyote that he was going to trust with his life. He thought that reading about other people made him feel connected and it made him feel safer. Connectedness is something that he needed now it was at the very core of his being, it was primal, so vital that he needed to respond to it, strongly, indifferently or weakly, subliminally always...but he needed to respond. He responded by allowing himself to think positive thoughts. But as he read, it became more difficult.

Iñaki Arrieta from Naco a tiny place on the Mexican border. The name deriving from the last two letters of Arizona and Mexico. The most infamous staging area to illegally cross the border into the U.S.

Iñaki was a double agent, and an ex-Militant Basque Separatist. Mark had gotten his name from reliable sources and assured Alex he could be trusted...for a price. $20,000 U.S. dollars up front.

It was much more than the going price but then again this was a special crossing. Instead of leaving Mexico to the U.S. he was to guide an American through the Yucatan peninsula through Central America, and into the mountains near Quito, Ecuador.

When Iñaki arrived in a dusty SUV, Alex still felt no connection. On the contrary, he did not like the look of the overdressed flashy man that came right up to him as if he was an old friend.

"Rodolfo... Rodolfo Blanco?" he asked.

"No, Mr. Blanco died in Texas, on Sunday." Alex replied.

There was a pause. Alex's hand was in his small duffel bag gripping his Glock.

"His widow Monica will miss him." The man said.

Alex thought for a moment, the correct reply was "misses him."

"Very well, do you have my papers?" he asked him reaching to shake his hand.

"I have everything, do you have my money?"

"Let's get going we'll take care of business in the car."

Alex felt that if he took the lead it would always keep the stranger on the defense.

"OK, let's go." He said leading the way.

In the car as they drove out of the parking lot of the Jose Marti Library, the assigned pickup spot Alex handed him $10K in one stack of hundreds. Before he released it from his grip he told him, "the other half when we get to Quito plus a $5K bonus."

"All right, I can live with that." He replied and he handed Alex a manila envelope in return.

They were now on a main road heading south as Alex went through the contents of the envelope. Inside were two passports. An American one in the name of Vincent Sanguinetti and a Mexican one in the name of Rodolfo Blanco.

"So what should I call you?" the smuggler asked him.

"Call my Rudy."

"We are going to cross into Guatemala and Honduras before we stop for gas. I presume you want to drive-on through with no stops. We can share the driving. Let's stop up ahead we'll switch and you can drive the next 4 hours and I will sleep, wake me a few miles from the border, don't forget I have to make sure to take care of the border agents. I presume you have a gun in your bag. It's Ok unless I tell you otherwise. I will make sure they don't search but if   they do decide to search go along with it. They will not arrest you; it will just mean a bigger bribe. $100 will take care of it, my cook made us sandwiches and drinks in the cooler back there, we should be in Quito in a couple of days."

There was something in the manner he carried himself, the way he acted that made Alex uncomfortable. He would dread going to sleep.

He drove quietly the next few hours thinking about it when it was his turn to sleep. After a while he stopped thinking and just drove.

When he passed the town of Sabancuy he knew from Iñaki's map that he was an hour away. He looked at his watch to wake his companion on time.

He shook him gently awake when the time came.

"Oh man," he yawned and stretched. "Damn good time, we are ten minutes from the border, pull up ahead and let's take piss break and switch."

There they were peeing on the side of the road and the Basque never stopped talking. Something about the Mexican government and how the prices of bribes were going up, etc. God how he loved the sound of his voice. Alex listened reluctantly.

When they approached the border a couple of guards made their way to the drivers side but before they could get there a fat guard came out of the small customs office and waved them away. He went right up to the Basque and exchanged greetings. They knew each   other. Iñaki handed him our passports. Folded in one of the passports were several bills. In less than a minute the guard came back and they were on their way.

There were no new customs stamps on their passports. They were never there.

As they drove away Iñaki gave Alex a quick wink with a big grin.

Alex did not feel any safer.

He did all he could to stay awake in the next few hours telling him that he was not tired. He tried at conversation with him to stay awake.

"What kind of a name is Iñaki?" He asked him even though he knew it was Basque.

"It's Basque. My father was born there, he came to Mexico when he was twenty and married my mother and they had me. He named me after his father a famous Jai Alai player. You know Jai Alai?"

"It's like tennis but with some sort of wicker racket, right?" Alex kept on with the charade.

"NO, NO, it's a "cesta", and it takes great skill to play." He said a bit disturbed.

"Do you play?" Alex asked him.

"Of course, every Basque plays, it's in our blood."

Alex smiled before he asked him point-blank.

"So why don't you play instead of this?"

"You want to know why I do it, it's the money!" he said to

Alex. "I make more money   doing this than when I was in Texas as a manager of a restaurant, and I tell you my friend that was a good job. But I had a couple of girlfriends on the side and my wife found out and filed for divorce and she made a lot of trouble for me, she got the judge to give her almost half my salary, I said the hell with that! I came back home and began to work as a "guide" and now I run 10 to 20 coyotes all by myself and make ten times what I made in Texas, and life down here is cheaper. I only go to Texas when I want to buy a car and bring it back to Mexico, like this baby here." He proudly tapped the console.

Alex listened to him for as long as he could. When he started talking about how much money it was costing him to bribe officials for the tenth time he began nodding off. Before he knew it he was dreaming of dolphins in the Ocean running beside his boat as he steered for the sunset.

When Alex awoke he was surprised to learn they were in Nicaragua. He had slept on and off through two countries in less than a day. He was alone in the car in front of some cantina. He went inside and went to the bathroom and tried to wash up on the filthiest sink he had ever seen. Afterwards, grossed out as he was he felt that he was hungry.

When he came out he went to a table wondering where the Basque was. An old man wearing a dirty apron came over and brought him a cold Corona and some tacos on a plate that had several edges missing, and where the ceramic pieces were missing the edges were dirty as if the plate had just been dug out of the ground, he took the   beer and drank thirstily. Then he looked at the plate again and ignored the plate, he just stared at the steaming corn tortillas filled with meat and some cheese and the savory sauce that was oozing from them. It smelled fantastic. As the saying goes when you are hungry you will eat a dead…whatever, he picked one up and stuffed half of it in one bite. The taste was heaven. Then the heat came on. He liked hot food. This was hot, really hot. But after a few bites and some more beer he finished both delicacies and wiped his mouth with his shirt sleeve.

The old man offered his dirty apron, grinning.

"Good, heh," then added, "your friend is getting laid upstairs."

Alex grinned at the thought.

"How much for everything including my friend's entertainment?"

"Twenty *pesos*."

He handed the old man a $100 bill and winked at him.

"*Muchas Gracias caballero!*"

There is nothing like money to raise your status in life he thought as he waited outside; downing another beer and thinking of what awaited him. He had not had time to think about his bleak future. But now was not the time. He finished the beer as he heard the boisterous Basque inside the tavern. Within minutes they were on the road again.

"Hey that was good of you to pay for my fun; you should have seen the ass on that Mayan bitch." He said stretching his arms wide.

Alex was driving and he had not gone a mile when Iñaki was fast asleep. He smiled and gunned the engine at the thought of a few hours of peace and quiet.

It went like this as they made their way down the Pan American Highway and on to Quito.

Iñaki brought him to the Old Intercontinental Hotel. He smiled as he accompanied him all the way to his room. Alex paid him and thanked him and told him that he wanted to sleep for a month.

"No problem, anytime my friend." Was the last thing he said shaking his hand.

After he left, Alex waited a half-hour and changed rooms. He was still not convinced about his new "friend".

Alexander
&
Illapa

"Love is composed of a single soul inhabiting two bodies."
--Aristotle

19

Quito, Ecuador two days later.

Quito the capital of Ecuador is the closest he would get to heaven he thought as he looked out of the balcony. He had opened the curtains and thought he might be dead already. As he looked out the sliding glass doors all he could see was clouds, clear out to the horizon. He drank more coffee and opened the doors and stepped out into the balcony and the early morning fog. The sight was incredible. The clouds surrounded the hotel just below his floor which was only the third floor of five story building. He looked over the railing and all was clouds. It was like in the movies. He thought he could just step over the railing and walk in the clouds. He stared in wonder for a long time until his concentration was broken by a figure two balconies away. She had just walked out to the railing and looked just as awed.

He saw that she was an Indian girl as she glanced at him without expression. She was wearing only a long T-shirt with the Inka Cola Logo that just covered her body above her legs. When she leaned on the railing the tail of the shirt rose up slightly and if her raven-black straight hair had been an inch longer it could have covered her where the shirt hem had failed but, alas, he stared at the base of her buttocks and he could see that she was naked underneath. He became very aroused looking at her perfect ass. He could not remember how long it had been since he felt such lust and caressed his growing erection discreetly inside his loose shorts.

She looked at the blanket of clouds for a good while and then at him again with the same blank expression. Alex would alternate looking at the clouds and at her, until he could take it no more and went inside to take a shower and put her out his mind.

No sooner had he finished cooling his rapture when her image appeared in the mirror as he combed his hair. He could see the exotic gorgeous features. High cheekbones, thin nose, and those perfect almond eyes. Were they actually blue or grey, they were light European eyes, for sure. It would be a restless night, he thought as she faded from his sight.

He had made the call to his contact the same day he arrived. He was told that it would take a few days to get everything organized. He did not like the idea of waiting around the hotel. When he told them   that he would make other arrangements, he immediately was told they would come the very next morning. Again he felt uncomfortable.

He ordered a club sandwich and a bottle of wine, just in case he got lucky with the exotic neighbor. Funny how men always plan these little scenarios as if they could by sheer will make them take place. He could go over and knock on her door and ask her to join him. No that would be too bold for him, besides he needed to keep a low profile. He ate alone and drank half the bottle and fell asleep listening to ESPN on the TV.

When the knock came at 5:15AM the next morning he was ready to go.

He opened the door and was greeted by a dark man.

"Mr. Blanco, my name is Rene, Iñaki sent me and I will be your guide."

He was dressed in a light-blue *guayabera*, smiled too much and seemed a bit casually dressed for the long haul ahead and besides it was too cool for just a shirt; Alex thought about Iñaki and felt the same uneasiness. But his judgment and thoughts were interrupted when he saw the beautiful girl from the balcony behind him. He said her name was Marta and looked away when his eyes met hers.

"*Señor* Blanco, we need to hurry to avoid traffic."
He picked up Alex's bag and led the way.

He was about to say something about the fact that there was no mention of another "client". But how could he object, after all she seemed harmless, and don't forget that delicious ass.

Looking   cautiously   about, Marta followed behind and hurriedly kept up the pace with the men. The early morning was dark, silent and refreshingly cool because of the altitude. They followed Rene to the alleyway on the side of the Hotel. A cat sprang from a trash pile and ran away into the darkness. The man, Rene seemed nervous. In the end of the alleyway he stumbled as he turned to make sure of where we were.

"Here is my Jeep and we need to move out fast." He loaded their bags hastily.

The passenger door of a car parked across the street from the Hotel was partially open and Alex who had scouted the hotel grounds as soon as he had settled in his room the previous night knew that it was a good spot for ambush, he could see two men coming out of the bushes towards them but he could not see if they were carrying weapons but he was sure one of them was Iñaki.

"Put your hands on the car roof!" Rene ordered holding a Baretta to Alex's face and forcing him against the car.

It took only a second, as this was all she needed. Rene turned to the girl to tell her to follow his orders. But in his Macho world he could not imagine that a mere woman was capable of the swift and calculated deadly move with a knife, for he barely got out the first syllable when she had plunged the short commando knife she carried in her belt buckle into his neck and across his jugular. He began to slip down the side of the car lifeless, but Alex held him up as a shield. The girl grabbed the Beretta from his dead hand. The two men realized what was happening, and aimed their guns; the girl fired three rounds from a crouching position. The first shot killing one instantly as it entered through his right eye. And the next two rounds hit Iñaki, one in the chest and the second grazed his left temple. They both fell. Iñaki got a round off that hit the dead Rene in the abdomen; he was aiming at Alex's chest. The girl walked over to the mortally wounded Basque trying to speak gasping and coughing blood.

"You fascist pig, this is for my people."

She fired a bullet into his mouth.

How did she know?

Alex was going over the wallet of the dead Rene, he was a local cop trying to cash in on the reward for the girl which was $200,000. Alex showed the girl the Interpol flyer.

He looked at the girl and she looked back at him.

"I need to go into the mountains to hide I can't explain it at the moment?" He said to her.

"I will go with you for now." She replied cool as ice.

They went back to the Jeep and as they drove past the parked car, Alex stopped and quickly got out of the Jeep and opened the driver's door, on the floor he recognized Iñaki's leather knapsack he took it and got back into the Jeep. Alex was driving and the girl next to him.

Alex gave a short laugh.

"What's so funny?" The girl said coldly.

"The way you shot the man in the mouth, that's where I would have shot him, he drove me crazy on the drive down here."

"Me too, he thought he could seduce me, the stinking Spanish pig."

"He was Basque."

"Same shit."

Alex could not read her expression, she was a cold one.

"Can you read a map?"

She nodded. He handed her a map of Quito and he pointed out the escape route he had chosen in case something or someone changed his original plan.

She studied the map and then told him calmly to take the next road east, towards the Colombian border.

"Why did you take his bag?"

"I didn't care for his services, I wanted my money back."

2 0

Ecuador/Colombia border a few hours later.

Alex did not stop until they were a few kilometers from the border with Colombia and then headed south to where they found a trail from the road and drove the Jeep in the dirt road until they hit another paved road that had a sign pointing north to the town of Tulcan in Colombia.

"My name is…" he hesitated, "Rudy".

"Marta"

No way, he thought if she is a Marta I'm a friggin' Eskimo. She stared with the same expression at the road ahead, with the Beretta on her lap   holding down the map.

"Listen, Mar-ti-ca, we might as well get to know each other we could be together for some time."

"Listen, Ru — dy, it's none of your fucking business, and I don't care who the hell you are, so you keep driving and if I catch you looking at my ass again I will shoot you in those roving eyes, *Comprende!*"

Someone had wound-up this bitch so tight, maybe he could dump her and go on by himself. Wait think it over, his mind was clearing now, she did save his life, and she is pretty handy with that knife and pistol. I'll wait. She must have been thinking along the same lines.

"Listen, machon, I don't like this anymore than you, I don't know you, nor do I want to, but it appears that we have the same problem. We both want to get to the mountains. Once there we go our separate ways, Ok?"

"Sure."

She was right of course. He thought he could barely make out a semblance of a smile. Both were thinking the same thing, once in the mountains, get rid of anyone or anything that could lead to their capture.

The town of Tulcan was announced by a wooden sign with more bullet holes than a slice of Swiss cheese.

In Tulcan they drove around quietly getting acquainted with the town. They drove by the police station, they both made mental notes as to how many, what kind of cars.

The girl sat quietly gauging him. Maybe he wasn't as

useless as he looked.

They drove back to a general store they had passed and Alex drove into their small parking lot and backed the Jeep into a spot against the wall of the store.

They went inside and were surprised to find it very well stocked with almost everything they needed. They went through the store picking out their various needs, he packed boxes of canned goods cooking utensils and condiments and she packed grooming needs and first-aid supplies. They paid for everything quickly and when they were loading the jeep a man approached them.

"Buenos dias, señor y señora." The older Indian began assuming they were husband and wife.

Paco.

Paco Lugo was a believer now, a good Christian. He was no longer a cocaine smuggler and hired killer. Padre Cruz had converted him when he tried to eliminate him. It is ironic how God works his miracles. Hired by the cartels to kill he ended up being saved.

Paco was a tall man for an Indian, looking more Italian, actually Sicilian or Greek, with dark thick wavy hair that once was very black. Now only a few strands of dark hair peeked out of the grey. His complexion was ruddy as if he had just come in from a day on the beach. His body heavy in the middle. But his arms and legs were powerful. He used to drink. A power drinker. Never stopping until   he dropped. Which was good because his size always intimidated his drinking buddies and no one wanted to mess with Paco when he drank. The thing that made Paco stand out was the sound of his voice. It came low and hoarse, from way down deep in his throat. It was there that they had almost destroyed his larynx during an emergency tracheotomy that saved his life after a bullet went through his neck. So as big and menacing as he was his words came out quiet, raspy and barely audible.

He had gone into Tulcan to visit a dying aunt who left him a house which he sold after she died. He was going back to the Village that he loved and where he had the family that he always wanted. Dominique had taken him in after his conversion. It took him months to get her to accept his proposal of marriage and another year before Padre Cruz would marry them. He remembered kissing his fiancé ten times that year before the wedding. At first frustrating and then a welcome release from the lustful prison of the flesh.

When at last he held his bride on his wedding night and made love to her. He cried like a baby. Thanking God for his good fortune in giving him another chance and forgiving his sins.

When he saw the young couple loading camping equipment, he assumed they were going into the mountains and he offered his services. He offered to buy their Jeep and they did not rule out the offer once they were through with their trip. His own jeep had broken down and he was thinking of how he would have to buy another for   the trip home. He was glad when he found them. They even offered to "rent" his Colombian license plates as they would offer less hassles in their travels through Colombia. When they offered $500 American dollars, he thanked God for his good fortune.

"Where are you going?" Paco asked innocently enough. There was an uneasy silence from the front seat.

The older man sat in the back eating an arepa and drinking from a clear bottle, Alex, hoped it was water, (which it was).

He glanced at the girl and she looked back at him searching for words.

"Paco, we are researchers looking for herbal cures and healing plants, we both work for The University of Salamanca in Spain, do you know of it?"

"Well…no I must admit I have not, I'm not an educated man, in the classroom, I mean, I was taught in the school of life. And thanks to God I have a good woman at home that is much smarter and better than me to keep me on the straight and narrow path."

"Where is home." The girl asked.

"The Village of Teruan, high in the mountains. A good five days journey if the roads are good. Perhaps you would like to come and visit me and my wife. We do not have much to offer but it is all yours. She knows the mountains like the palm of her hand and can tell you where to find what you are looking for. Please come we would love to have you."

Alex looked at the girl   and she just looked at him with a face that said; *don't stop now you're on a roll!* So he continued.

"Paco we will go with you as far as Teruan and then we will decide where to go from there."

"Very good", said the old man.

They covered very little ground the rest of the day. The dirt road that Paco had directed them to take was full of pot holes and mud, but it was secluded and they had not seen another car since they passed the last farm a good hundred miles back.

At nightfall the old man led them to a nice clearing where they set up camp for the night.

When the old man saw that Alex was looking at instructions for the raising of the tent he began to grin.

But after a short while they had pitched their tent and the old man set up a sleeping bag with a lean-to covering his head and went to sleep by the nice fire he had made.

In the morning he was once more puzzled and realized that the man and woman had a strange relationship. They had slept in the same tent but hardly made any sounds. He awoke to the animated voice of the girl.

"Look you perverted bastard, if you rub yourself against me one more time I'm going to cut your dick off!"

"Hey, don't get so touchy, I was asleep and I didn't mean to rub against you… in that way, it was an accident."

Alex was still talking as he crawled out of their tent,

completely dressed. The old   man just laughed to himself.

The girl followed behind also dressed and moved past him and made her way to the woods nearby.

"Women!" Alex said shaking his head at the old man and whispering to himself *"bitch!"*

"Yes my young friend, they are something, aren't they?"

"You can say that again."

"I think you have a live one there."

Alex did not reply just moved away in the opposite direction she had taken.

Paco assumed they were not a couple but colleagues.

They couldn't be police, they were too innocent, he thought.

On the second day they drove until late afternoon in the same unpaved road that had gotten drier and they made some good time. Paco suggested they stay in an abandoned village that had one serviceable house. House was stretching it. It was built of wood, it was a nice house at some point with wooden planks on the outside covering the inside frame made up of logs. The roof leaked but there was no sign of rain so they got a fire started.

"Im going to find us some fresh meat." Paco offered. "There are wild pigs by the stream towards the rear of the house. I shot one when I last stayed here."

"No, I will go." Alex said very confidently.

She looked at the old man with a thin smile.

The old man got the message.

"All right, look for the   pits in the ground and any sound in the bushes, but be careful they are very aggressive."

Alex took his pistol, the one the dead Basque used to try to kill him, a Smith and Wesson 357 Magum with a medium barrel, and looked to see if it was loaded. The girl watched him carefully.

Alex was sure of himself as he handled the gun, he felt its weight in his hands, aimed it once, then again at the girl across the room, who narrowed her eyes in defiance, and then he thrust it into his waistband and began to walk out.

"Hey machon," she mocked him, "better take a knife in case you miss, you can always cut his throat, you know, it's beneath the head and just under his tusks."

The old man dared not laugh; he held back and just looked down at the floor.

With her eyes following him Alex walked out of the cabin, he wanted to shoot her, but he just kept on walking, thinking that the knife was a good idea, but there was a snowball's chance in hell he was going back to get it.

He made his way around the house and began walking towards the stream which he figured was in the clearing just ahead about a quarter mile. As soon as he saw the stream he heard rustling in the bushes. He crouched low and pulled his revolver and cocked it. He moved slowly towards the noise. He began to think about the knife again. Damn the bitch he thought.

From his left the rustling became louder and a grunting sound came with it. He tried to see through the heavy weeds, he moved to one side for a better   vantage, and then he saw the wild boar. It was almost black with mud or clay splotches all over his body. The beast saw him also and charged him, teeth glaring grunting and shaking his head up and down, it was then he saw the curling tusks on either side of his mouth. He aimed and squeezed the trigger. The recoil of the powerful gun sent him reeling on his ass. The pig kept coming, he missed. He tried for one more shot but the pig was almost on him. Then he heard the shot. It came from behind him. The pig twisted in mid-air and came down grunting at his feet, blood gushing from his head and mouth.

He looked around and there she was crouching holding her Beretta with both hands aiming it at his head.

He froze.

A faint smile began to form on her mouth. She raised her gun and released the pin. She slid it into the holster on her hip.

"You should use an automatic, it will give less recoil."

She came to him and offered her hand to help him up.

He ignored her and walked away shaking the dirt from his pants.

Paco was nodding his head behind her, holding a knife in his right hand.

The old man went to the pig and began to carve him. He came into the house carrying a hind quarter.

Later the girl had gone to bathe in a stream nearby. Alex had placed the hind quarter of the pig in a big iron kettle and added beer and spices and wild vegetables and left it cooking.

He turned to the old   man who had been watching him urging him to use more chilies.

"Leave it covered for at least an hour. I'll be back before then."

He started to walk outside but the old man grabbed his arm.

"Look son, that woman out there has something bothering her, I know that kind of pain, go easy on her. She has feelings for you. Before she shot the pig, she told me she was going to make sure you were all right."

"We'll see."

He went to the stream and watched her as she bathed. Paco smiled when he saw where he was. He left them alone and went inside and poked at the pig roasting that was beginning to send an aroma reminding him of home and he smiled and added more chilies.

The girl saw him watching her. She forced back a smile. She was aware of what she was doing. Every move, each caress with her hands as she touched her body was a code. When she found herself in a state of arousal she turned towards him. Exposing herself completely. The eyes. The cold predatory eyes. The same eyes that elicited fright. Now beckoned with lust and want.

Alex looked for a few seconds but felt embarrassed and then turned and walked away upstream.

He sat by the water's edge on an old log that had been there for a long time well anchored to the land by the stubs of once mighty branches. He thought about the future. What lay ahead? The last few days seemed a blur in his memory, no time to think. He needed to make some sort of plan. But his head raced and all he could see in front of his eyes was her naked body.

After a while with only more questions and no answers, he made his way back to the cabin.

She was in her folding bed combing her hair. There was something new in her face, it was softer. She looked up at him continuing to brush, then away.

"Hey my friend, you are a good cook, the pig is perfect and tasty." Said the old man.

"I'm famished." She said.

"Then let's eat." He said.

The old man began to carve meat that needed no carving, as it came off the bone easily. It was moist and steamed as he served them on a rustic table, that he had set up with a kerosene lamp in the middle.

The old man had added some root vegetable that appeared to be a potato, but on tasting proved to be sweet and Alex figured it was a local sweet potato, and of course it had some heat from the chilies he had sneaked in.

The girl had begun to cut some of her meat when the old man clasped his hands and began to pray.

"Dear Lord please bless these gifts from thy bounty, always provide for those less fortunate that do not have food, and bless our family, friends and even our enemies, reach down into their hearts and change   them, in Jesus name we ask. And Lord bless my friends Rudy and Marta as they make their way into the mountains, guide them, watch over them. Amen."

Alex clasped his hands and Illapa crossed herself.

"Hmmm this is good." She said through a mouthful of food. "Well at least you can cook, Machon."

Alex looked at her semblance of a smile and forced a thin smile back.

"Hah, Hah, Hah. Gracias a Dios, (Thanks be to God)." The old man beamed.

After the meal Alex went to his cot and studied the map of the region.

Illapa went outside.

"Hey, why don't you take her gun to her, there may be an angry hog out there looking for his dead mate or some Jaguar that is looking for the carcass." He handed Alex her gun in the holster.

He went outside to look for her.

After walking towards the road, he found her leaning against the Jeep with her arms crossed looking straight at him.

"Thought you might need this."

"Thanks."

He walked around for a bit trying to find the right words.

"What's on your mind Ru—dy?"

He looked at her sarcastically.

"You know it's not my name."

"Ok, so what."

"My name is Alex, *Alejandro Dionisio Garcia*, I'm a fugitive from America. I cannot go back; there is a price on my head."

"Life's a bitch".

"I'm tired of lies; I have no idea where I am or where I'm going. That old man in there has the answer to his life in all his simple ways. He knows exactly where he is, who he is and where he is going…to his loving family and the waiting arms of his wife."

She looked at him not quite sure of what to feel she was puzzled, it made her anxious. He went on.

"I think you are like me, I don't want to know the details, but you know that a trail to us is dangerous, you are waiting for the right moment to eliminate all traces to you." He looked into her eyes now.

"What I have to say to you is: it doesn't have to be like that. I've been thinking and I'm going to take the old man's invitation and visit his village. Afterwards, well *It's blowing in the wind*, I'll cross that bridge later. All I ask is that you let us go and take the Jeep and whatever else you need and go on your way, you don't even have to tell us when, just go in the night or whenever."

"What do you think you'll find in the old man's village?"

"Perhaps some peace, I don't know, but I know I'm not a loner, perhaps I can do some good for his people. But I do know I want to rest for awhile. My life has been chaotic to this point; I want some peace and tranquility."

"I'm not going to kill   you or the old man. Heck, I didn't want to shoot the pig, but I thought he was going to hurt you."

She looked away still unsure of herself, this was very new to her. Why was she feeling she could trust him?

"Maybe I can go with you for little while and try to find some peace that sounds good."

It took a minute to register with Alex. He felt the same uneasiness. But he managed to nod and when he looked at her he could see a smile escaping from her lips.

The wall of fear and distrust that had kept them apart was crumbling under the spell of the evening mist that surrounded them. Like the clouds on the day they first saw each other it spread out before them and after a while they walked through it back to the cabin.

The Next Day.

It would be noon before they packed everything and resumed their trip.

The old man had a grin on his face. He knew something changed between them the previous night, he felt pretty good about himself right about now.

Something did happen, and they all knew it and acknowledged it in their own way.

Illapa hummed a tune from her ancestors. Alex would

look at her now and again. She was very helpful in packing and offered no criticism or coldness. Instead she offered the old man her favorite knife, the one that sliced Rene's neck in Quito.

Once when she bent down to pick up a bag her hair fell over her eyes, both her hands were carrying something, Alex saw it and came to her and brushed the loose strands out of her face. She looked him in the eyes and they spoke volumes.

In the car as the old man slept, Alex smiled at her and she smiled back.

Thankfully Paco said they should stop soon because he thought it would rain.

He offered to drive and let them rest.

They had traveled through unpaved back roads up to this point. Paco turned into paved road and his passengers looked at him.

"I want to take you someplace. A place that you might enjoy seeing," and "feeling," he added softly.

"Feeling?" Alex asked from the back seat.

"Yes, you will feel it when you see it."

Alex looked at the girl and she looked back. She shrugged an Ok to him.

The soaring spires were the first thing they saw. They then came around a bend in the road and they saw the church. The cathedral in Las Lajas in the southwestern mountains of Colombia sits on the side of a sheer cliff clinging to the land with fairy tale splendor. Out of the jungle, a thing of beauty, a pilgrimage   shrine   offering   hope and faith to the fortunate souls who break their life journey and visit.

Alex and the girl were looking in awe as Paco spoke.

"I always come here when I am close by, I come and pray and give thanks for my life, for all the good things that God has given me. I think you should go inside and walk around for a while and then we can go on."

"OK,"

There were very few words spoken for there was no need to communicate that which the heart sees. Around the church people of all races mingled. There was no class or political division. They all moved easily and peacefully. Some took pictures others drank and ate. Many were sick and crippled. But no one seemed anxious or in a hurry. Alex and the girl were separated for a short while. They reunited inside the church. They looked at the ornate altar with the Jesus on the cross. It was a peaceful few minutes as they took it all in.

"Isn't it beautiful." Said Paco as he handed each a rosary made of wood.

"A souvenir, for luck on your trip."

They made their way to a small clearing and had a picnic. As they ate they stole glances at each other. There was a familiar feeling being shared by both.

Paco said he was going to take a nap and proceeded to nod off.

They laid on the soft grass receiving the sun's warming rays and rested. After a while Alex began to tell her about his life, for something inside him   moved him. The memories far too long repressed. Now became impossible to quell. He remembered it well; it was all so very good where he was born.

He Reminisced.

"Our house was built right on the edge of the beach. It was my father's father who built it. He was good with tools, not at all like my father and me. They say he used to work all day on the house without a break, his only "helper" was a rum *mojito* supplied by my grandmother. He built it on the beach because of the breeze. *"In this land of endless sunshine"*, as he used to say, the cool gulf breeze made the days and nights tolerable. He used to sit in the porch at night with his "helper" nearby. It was not hard to figure the porch was his favorite part of the house. It was as if he built it for a purpose. It was small compared to the other houses."

My hand, outstretched, reached the sea.
All was green palms, quite near,
A pebble-strewn beach.
To the right and afar.
Curved a finger of land
With houses and churches, all facing towards me.
I could linger forever at this.
My first window
But the salt-spray is heavy
And time has no pause.

The words were coming back.

"When he was working at the bank he had met and befriended one of his clients. Anibal De La Cruz who had made some money and had been elected to the House of Representatives for a district that included the small fishing village of Jaimanitas, just west of Havana. Anibal had invited him to come spend a day at the beach house he had built on some land that the Government was about to distribute under a land-reform act. Anibal had taken a big chunk for himself and offered a couple of building lots to his new friend. My grandfather told him all he needed was a small lot to build his small home. My father would always remind him he should have taken the other lot as well. But my grandfather would not hear of it. He did not need more. Let someone else enjoy the sea alongside us. Within months my father would begin bringing in the materials needed and my grandfather built his house. He built it of wood two stories high. Big enough for two families. On the second story were the sleeping quarters. In the bottom the living area. And of course in front facing the Atlantic and overlooking our beach he built his porch.

The wooden railing surrounding it was at just the right height so that he could prop his feet on it as he sat on his favorite chair. From his porch he would look out to sea and try to find all the lights that belonged to the ships that sailed by. *"There you see, that one over there"* he would say to me whenever I wandered near to him, he would grab me and sit me in his lap *"That's an oil freighter, probably 100,000 tons   going west probably on its way to Mexico or Mariel Harbor."* I could hardly see the lights but I imagined the biggest ship I could and smiled at him.

What I remember most was his tanned rugged face with the probing dark eyes and his hair, that was pure white and never quite perfectly combed, and his strong hands and arms. He preferred to wear an old comfortable t-shirt and some cotton twill Bermudas that had long since their best. But his worn clothes smelled new, and clean and fresh like the ocean breeze.

In those days the smaller Cuban beaches were always full of Cubans. From Grandfather's porch you could see clear down to the pier on the east and to the beach club on the west. Our beach, as we called it, was neither big nor fancy, but it had all those wonderful qualities which make a good beach. The sand was light and pure and the water clear and warm.

Our beach was divided in two sections there was, of course, the common section next to the pier. Here was the best sand and very little rocks. And then the beach extended about a quarter-mile further up where there were parking spaces. You could sunbathe here along with all the city folk and the very few tourists.

During the summer something was always going on; baseball on the sand, or volleyball or just playing catch, we rarely ventured onto the public beach unless to play. We preferred the smaller strip of beach right in front of our house. It was private and made us proud because it was ours.

My grandfather taught me to swim on this beach; he

always boasted that I swam before I walked. And when I learned to walk I would just cross the narrow dirt road in front of the house and wade into the Ocean. He told me that sometimes I would jump from one of the steps with arms outstretched, like Superman and swim like a fish. And I was not yet two.

Every once in a while on some preordained mornings my grandfather would take me walking on the beach during peak tourist season. He would walk me past the tourists and the locals as they sunbathed or lay chatting or eating. I was just a toddler when this ritual started. He would take me down to the end where there was a pier that extended out about a hundred feet. There were usually some tourists on the pier snapping pictures and doing what tourists do. Here the fun started, my grandfather always began the ritual the same way. *"You have been such a bad boy I cannot put up with you any longer, I am going to throw you to the sharks!"* I would make believe that I was crying, *"No No, please help me!!!.* A short well-staged chase around the pier would arouse more looks and stares. Then he would pick me up, swing me back and forth a couple of times and throw me off the pier to the water below. People ran up to him screaming *"No No!!!"* All hell would break loose. Women shrieked, children inched closer over the edge to watch, and men shouted menacingly at my grandfather who just stood there with a grin on his face. And then just as suddenly as the commotion had started, my head would come bobbling out of the surface and I would be smiling broadly. My grandfather's laughter was the only thing you could hear amidst the shocked silence. He would still be laughing as he jumped in to join me and   together we would expertly swim away. The crowd, some smiling, some angry, slowly went back to doing what they were doing. I remember this one tourist, a very fat man in a floral shirt muttering to his wife, *"Damn these Cubans and their sense of humor"!* Alex smiled at the memory and glanced at her and caught her smiling for the first time. She was radiant.

This was the place where Alexander was born and raised for the first 9 years of his life. Where he spent a childhood that was later interrupted, and where he first learned about life, with his beloved family, especially his grandfather who meant so much to him. But soon he would also learn about the darker side of life, the side about evil, loss and displacement.

He was the best man he ever knew, but he was too young and did not have the time to tell him. He loved him dearly. He loved his lust for life, his patriotism, the way he moved his ears without moving his face. In the end there was no time to tell him. *But time has no pause.* The day would come when he would die. And now as an adult Alex realized how his memory kept him alive in his heart. He still wished he had told him how much he meant to him. *But time has no pause.*

Somehow, with a few simple words he could force back time and he would tell him and he would listen.

"My dearest grandfather you are the light of my life. The spark that brought to life everything inside me that is good. I miss you and yet I know you are here with me always."

Alex's Grandfather.

His grandfather was born in 1878, in the very heart of rural Cuba. Both his parents had come from the Canary Islands to work for a wealthy Spaniard. They worked his lands, sharecropping and working his farm. He never finished school. After 5th or 6th grade, he went to work with his parents on the farm. But he read every book his father gave him and some that he borrowed from their Landlord. His favorites, included Jules Verne, H. G. Wells, and Kipling.

These were turbulent times for Cuba. The growing revolt against Spain was on the rise. He would be swept up in the valiant struggle when he was 16. He went to war with the Mambi's (Cuban guerrillas) under the command of the legendary leader Antonio Maceo.

Maceo's charisma inspired him to fight. He was not a brave man nor did he consider himself a patriot. He was doing his duty for his country, the country of his birth.

During one of the campaigns the regiment was camped near the sea at the port of San Miguel in the western tip of the island. Here the supply ships laden with American arms and aid would supply the small army of patriots. As he looked out to sea his heart stirred. Thus began a lifelong love that would bring him to our beach.

Maceo spoke to him once when he was walking on the beach. He had wandered a distance from the camp and before he knew it a small group made its way to him. He immediately recognized the mulatto leader.

"*Muchacho*, "Kid", what are you doing this far from camp?"

He told the great leader that he loved to walk on the beach. Maceo asked for his name and where he was from. After some kind words for his family and hometown he told him that now was the time to fight, the time would soon come to walk on the beach…in freedom.

What a man, he thought, this is a true patriot, the best of men, brave, intelligent and born leader.

Would he know then how it would end he would have warned him, told him of the perils and prejudices of his fellow man. But then he could not see the future. And history would write the sad chapter of what could have been for his new country if one as Maceo had been its first president and the father of his country.

But time has no pause.

Many years later when he was an older man, he would be confronted by government representatives that wanted to give him a pension for his war service. It was an overdue effort to appease the true patriots, the *mambises* of the war for Independence. He had told them then with words that were inspired by Maceo, "I did not fight for money, I fought for freedom for Cuba."

He was alone now; both his parents had died before the turn of the new century and he was free to choose his own way in life. With very little money he decided on a career in banking.

A friend introduced him to   the Manager of a local bank in rural town and he became a teller. He worked his way up to Manager.

He met my grandmother and romanced her in the custom of the times with love letters. He once showed me the letter that won her heart. The first time I read it I could not make heads or tails of it. I was too young, the language and words did not make sense to me. I realize today that it was a wonderful letter, full of love and admiration. The way it was in those days.

Adriana:

There are two glorious moments that have given me infinite Joy. One was the first time I saw you, the second was yesterday. From the first moment I saw you I felt a wonderful feeling of unabashed happiness. But yesterday was unforgettable as my hopes and dreams were realized and I tasted for the very first time the sweet fruits of love. In all reality I must confess that you may still have your doubts. But I must tell you how deeply and ardently I love you. I tremble at my boldness in writing you these words. And know that with one word you could shatter all my hopes and dreams. But if you were to tell me that you feel the same, that you could love me. I would find the courage to face your father, and all your family and to beg for their approval and blessing.

I am a new man, a hopeful fortunate man, kneeling at the altar asking God to bless you and guide me to win your heart. I pledge my heart and soul to make you happy and give you all that your heart desires.

Please write me   and tell me how you feel. You know my heart. Let me know yours.

Yours until death,
Jose M G.

By the time Alex was born the old man had mellowed. With age and wisdom came a totally new perspective on life. Above all he remembered how full of life he was. He was a terrific man. No one in the family ever came close to his charm and vitality.

He was admired by his friends, he had no enemies. He was the type of man you wanted as a friend. He was a contented, quiet and sincere individualist who beckoned life head-on with optimism. In the midst of loud, proud egotists that so often make up the Cuban scene.

Alex never realized that he was so old when he sat with him in the balcony as a young boy. *But time has no pause.* He had lived his life so full. But he could not have known this until it was too late to talk to him about all these things. He had to rely on the conversations with his mother. She filled in the gaps.

His mother told him that he told her once that men and women live their lives in two stages. In the first half of your life and the second. My grandfather had gone to war at 16. Alone in the world in his twenties, raised a family and built a home by the sea all before he was forty. His life had been lived in the first half.

Alex on the other hand was in his early 30's a failed marriage no children and for five years a killer and terrorist now hiding from the world. He was now sure there had to be another life out there for him. His mother's words haunted him. He began to hope in a future.

Alex realized he began to see the world with cynicism when his grandfather died that winter in Cuba. A couple of years later he would be uprooted to a new country and all the effort and blood that his grandfather had shed for his country were forgotten. His beloved Cuba was in the hands of a tyrant much worse than Spain. A homegrown tyrant, a Cuban who hated not loved. Alex was glad his beloved grandfather did not live to see this.

A Few Days Later.

They set up camp very quickly, Paco thought to himself. Then Illapa said she wanted to find the stream that they had seen from the road. Alex watched her go until she disappeared from sight.

"She left her gun again." Alex said it picking up the gun and holster.

The old man just looked at him and winked.

"What are you waiting for…GO!"

Alex walked briskly after her.

She was standing by the stream in a nice clearing she had

placed her towel on the soft   grass and had taken off her pants and when she saw him looking at her she gently unbuttoned her shirt and slipped it off her shoulders, looking at him all the time.

Alex came to her and took her in his arms.

When he kissed her she felt a warm overwhelming warmness throughout her body. First with her lips, then her face and then her breasts. An electric current turned on for the first time in her life. She felt her whole being aglow from the touch of his lips to hers. She craved more.

Like her mother before her, she gave herself to a man that was completely enraptured with her.

They made love. They shared love. They whispered and shared sweet words and sighs of ecstasy. The girl for the first time in her life and Alex for the first time since he started to blot out his past.

2 0

Colombian Highlands, next day.

How does one express love to another human once you have expressed it before to someone else? You must question which one was the true love. If you lose a person you love through death, does not the love remain? Love lasts forever, even through death if you believe in heaven.

How can one person love more than once? Even if he or she abandon's you, hurts you or leaves you for someone else. Does not your love for that person remain with you forever? If Love is not eternal, then what is the use of saying to someone that you love them?

Is not God's Love eternal and perfect?

If we are truly God's   children then God made us imperfect when it comes to Love. But if you believe that we were perfect then why do we make so many mistakes for the sake of Love?

Alexander Dionisio Garcia pondered these questions as he stood in the stream near a cypress tree with its long roots twice the size of a man reaching down into the shallow water. He could see fish swimming around the brown columns in their water home. How perfect they seemed, how good they worked together this huge tree and its roots with the fish.

He was troubled in thought. Could he have been immoral in his love for Linda? Was this the real love? These feelings he felt up here in the mountains far from everything he knew. Far from the world he once shared with his family and friends and everyone that he cared for. For here in this place he felt the presence of a higher force for the very first time in his life.

She came to him and took his hand and led him away on the bank of the stream. She would look up to his face from time to time and blush. She would look away. But she would come back and look at him again.

"I Love You." She said.

"How do you know?" Alex asked softly.

They held each other for awhile until she spoke at last.

"My name is Illapa."

"Illapa." He repeated softly.

"I was born in Peru, my mother's lineage goes back hundreds of years to the ancient Incas. She was the daughter of

Kusi Tupac, a tribal leader.   My mother was a princess. She was kidnapped by my father who was a Colonel in the Peruvian Army but his family came from France. He was bewitched by the spirits when he saw her bathing in a stream, like this one here." She ran her hands through the water letting her fingers caress the stream and the words kept flowing freely like the current beneath them.

Alex was under her spell, all he could do was listen, listen with his heart.

"My father was a good man fighting a bad cause. But he loved my mother. He brought her back to our Village and asked for her hand in marriage. For a while he was a man of the people. He was respected. But his destiny was not allowed to be fulfilled. He was influenced by his leaders who were playing the usual political games. They used his marriage when convenient and in the end he was ordered to abandon his heart and family for politics. I hated him for choosing life over love. He was killed by my Guerrilla unit two years ago. I lived with my mother and grandfather for awhile and found out who I am. My mother told me she forgave him before she died."

They walked in silence for little while longer.

"Alex, I did many horrible things in my life, I have killed men and women and slept with men I did not love. I had to leave my country because I put my friend's lives in jeopardy. I don't blame you if you decide to leave me, for I could not live if anything ever happened to you because of me."

She reached up and kissed him. He held her and

whispered in her ear.

"Everything will be all right." And then added, "I have never felt like this before."

"I know." She said.

Alex nodded and began to talk in a low tone.

"You cannot imagine how alike we are. My father was killed by the very same people I joined to terrorize the world. And I did it for him. I thought I was fighting for a just cause. To liberate my country. But my father stood in the way, all he wanted was to achieve the same but in peace with love rather than hate. I ended up being the very creature he despised. My mother killed herself after my father died. Everyone including me thought she had gone insane. But now I know she did it for love. For love of the only man she ever loved. And I went out and became a terrorist to avenge their death. What I did was smear their perfect love with the blood of the innocents. I also have killed without mercy. And for it not for a friend I would not be here today, like you hiding from my past."

They made love one more time in the shallows of the stream. Two mere mortals wanting to transform themselves into another world. Like the fish swimming around them. OH, if only they could become them and swim away into the water world, where they could become something else. If only they could be reborn into another time and place.

The Next Morning.

    Paco was always the first to rise in the morning. He moved around the campsite checking for animals and tracks. During the night he had heard strange sounds; moaning and shrieks. He rustled the nearby brush.

    The sounds of the wild animals foretold of the rain. There was so much rain throughout the night that the stream overflowed to within yards of their tents. Paco had put plastic bags on his feet to walk to the car that was in a low area and the water had risen up past the exhaust pipe. But the car started and he moved it to higher ground.

    He washed his unshaven face in the cool water from the stream and brushed his teeth with the toothpaste Alex had given him. Then he went to the small alcohol Coleman two burner stove and lit the flame. Poured the coffee into the kettle and did not bother to measure as Alex had asked. The coffee would be strong like he liked.

    When the coffee was done Alex came out of the tent, stretching lured by the scent.

    Paco poured each a cup. He took his black; Alex with two spoonfuls of sugar.

    Paco looked at Alex and studied his face for a while. There was something strange. The eyes. Alex's eyes they glowed with life. Sparkled like the sun's rays streaking through the tall oaks to their left. Yes, there was something in his eyes. The way he drank his coffee. He savored the strong blend. He was quite content this morning sitting beside the   older wiser mountain man.

When at last Paco looked at him for a clue, Alex looked back. A mischievous grin on his face. As his college roommate from Alabama used to say. "A possum-eatin shit grin."

All Paco could do was smile back remarking;

"Hey my brother you look at peace with the World?"

"*Si, si*...it's been a long time but right now I am at peace with the World, and every single thing and person in it!"

"*Gracias a Dios*". Paco offered.

"Yes, praise him, indeed, for he made woman didn't he?"

"Si, si."

"I have a wonderful wife waiting for me at home. I would like it very much if you would meet her, she is my angel, I do not deserve her, but God has been kind to me."

"So you are a religious man?"

"*Si*, I am here today but for the grace of God." Paco crossed himself.

Paco told the young man about his past and of the priest.

"I would like to meet this priest someday."

"*Si*, I will take you to him, he is English you can talk to him about anything, and he's truly a man of God."

"So how much longer to your village?"

"Another day, with good weather."

"Then let's get going, I will get the Princess."

Paco was going to smile at the sarcasm, but Alex said it so matter-of-factly that he just nodded.

21

The Village of Teruan, Colombia a few weeks later.

It was blue, yes blue, the sky. With clouds, few but white. Up there, the world was clean and bright and radiant, a radiant blue; it was always blue, the sky. What a wonderful day to be alive!

It was fearful and grim on the footpath in the hills near the Village. But after you reached the clearing just before the Village, the high mountain air that is clean, fresh and pure, invigorated your lungs and spirit. And the sky was blue. It was not unlike a pilgrimage with the roads less traveled a necessary means to reach a glorious end.

It was Christmas; they would spend the night Making Hallacas, Illapa, Alex and Dominique. They would be delicious. It took a while for him to notice, but when he realized himself that something was happening, he saw it first. Illapa's eyes had changed. She would look at Alex from time to time with a new face. It was softer and warm, engaging, as a breath of fresh air, a whisper of hope in the turmoil of their recent lives. Her eyes were an oasis of innocence. They had both survived the trial of their actions and now "bruised and battle worn" they hoped for something new, something better.

Alex thought that all the people he knew had by now the impression that he was a fascist-criminal totally out of control and totally mixed-up. Definitely mixed-up he thought. Even now he felt out of control again. But at this moment he did not care. The troubles of the world he felt could not be solved with Love. He figured someone or group would always take it to the extreme and use the trust and Love of man for his or their benefit. Somehow in this remote place he began to re-think about the good in mankind. He always knew that there are truly good people on earth, like his Grandfather. But he had given up searching them out. All the bloodshed and killing was a by- product to him. It was irrelevant to him, he knew his country of birth was fighting, therefore he would fight. But he also had a strong will to live. He sensed this in Illapa. But were he and Illapa really fighting for an ideal or were they fighting for some mysterious cause. When you came right down to it he was beginning to realize they were fighting for themselves. Like most of the world. Their violent acts made in the guise of an ideal replaced the love for their fellow man. Their total repudiation of romantic ideals of Love and Faith and Hope was their crime. A history of violence changes men and women. Only divine intervention can bring them back. But the recognition of true love and good can be illusive to those who choose to close the eyes of their heart.

The fruit was ripe and ready to eat, mangoes, chirimollas, guavas and more. Harvest time was at hand. And they ate their food and fruit fresh and warm under a shady tree. The juices flowed from their lips as they smacked and lapped their tongues savoring the nectar. It was a wonderful time of silence and knowing glances. Just a few hours next to a vibrant, young woman totally devoted to goodness. Her essence of purity and sanctity touching their souls.

Dominique was small in stature and when she moved around the room surrounded by her aura of humility she almost became insignificant. But when you looked closely you would see a strikingly beautiful exotic young woman with black hair and sad teddy bear eyes that never quite gazed directly at you.

There was a small scar on her   nose and two along her lips. But the beauty of her maple colored skin that glowed with the embers of the small fire in the hut hid them well. As for the mental scars she bore throughout her life they were also hidden, no... healed, when she found her soul and heart in the jungle that was her home.

And then Dominique ushered Paco and all their children and some others under her care and in her small makeshift dining room sat the large group down to dinner with a prayer.

"My Lord Jesus guide them, watch over us and all who dwell in your house. They are my... your angels. Bless them with your presence and salvation. We are not perfect in our lives but we are perfect in your holy eyes. Thanks, Thanks for taking our sins unto your body, Thanks, Thanks for taking our pain, the salvation of the World rests on your body and spirit. You are our savior. Thanks for my faith, it is not perfect, but it is mine. Amen".

Alex and Illapa two fugitives from a World of their fathers almost at once felt themselves part of another World. They both felt self-conscious and anxious. Yet there was a connection.

They thanked Dominique and Paco for the food. Illapa embraced her and whispered words that Alex and Paco could not understand but they sensed their meaning. And they walked away into the jungle which had somehow lost its dread and portentous nature and beckoned them for the short hike to the hut they now called home.

As they passed through the Village how avidly they

scanned the scene, two old men playing checkers so serene. An upturned box for a table and a bucket and tree stump for chairs. A fantastic incongruity with the youth and life that teemed around the center of the small village. Beyond the center or "village square". Children played. Had they stayed there in the midst of the villagers cushioned among them like faceless tourists gawking at their quaintness with fear, they might have returned that very night to reality, to what they were. But a question festered on their minds. What did they live for? Killing and mayhem? Or perhaps tomorrow's sip of the bitter wine of persecution and guilt. No matter, they lived, and that was all that mattered. To live with them, to be like them! Desire burned within their souls. Desire burned within the man and woman — this was the culmination of the magic. Towards this their hearts raced. They turned, resolved and happy and here was something new, dark and mysterious as their past but quiet and inviting. Gingerly, they moved eager for the first contact with the people. They were offered tea. They drank from empty cans, the steaming liquid soothing on their tongues. And they relaxed and smiled. The night sky was dark and cloudy devoid of stars. But they saw blue. It would always be blue. Around them on the village they saw their new friends laughing, gesturing, and walking in brilliant splendor. The walls of hate were crumbling. They still remembered, but for them the sky was blue. The rose-colored glasses would stay, they vowed, forever. Fatal vow, foolish vow, how long, how long forever is?

A Few Nights Later.

He kissed her softly but she met his lips eagerly. He squeezed her body even closer to him and kissed her passionately overpowering her own kiss and after an eternity he let her go and looked at her with wonder and awe. But she could only gaze at him with half-closed eyes still lost in her passion and wanting more of him.

He took control. Kissing her neck and shoulders pulling her dress straps revealing more of her. He brought her close to him again and held her tenderly. Her soft words and phrases were in Quechuan and he did not understand them but he knew them like the tides of the Ocean. With every inch of her body she spoke to him, knowingly, tenderly.

His unfilled heart pierced by arrows of faith and love, the wounds healing with the redemptive blood of Hope.

In this natural act of love, two lost souls became one. One heart, one pulse one release. Nothing and everything all at once. Wanting no end, yet knowing its imminent advent.

She began softly murmuring his name, *"Alejandro, Alejandro mi amor...mi vida*, My Love, My life"

He covered her face with endless kisses.

He lifted her in his arms, but he felt that she was lifting him to heaven on the arms of an Angel. His new heart was pumping the renewed blood to keep him conscious and breathing. It was all he could do to remain in control. At last the words came in a whisper, a   pleading to the Goddess that lay beneath, above, inside, and all around him.

"*Mi Amor Mi Vida*" My Love, my life, I love you with all my heart and soul"

Myles

"Do you wish to rise? Begin by descending. You plan a tower that will pierce the clouds? Lay first the foundation of humility". -St. Augustine (354-430)

22

Parkes, Australia 1981

The priest was Australian by birth. As a young man all he wanted to be was an actor. He saw Lawrence of Arabia and was captivated by Peter O'Toole's portrayal of Lawrence. He loved movies and watched them countless times. His father scolded him for wasting his time. But he knew better.

He became an outstanding athlete to keep his father off his back. Rugby and movies ruled his youth. He also read books, at first only those that interested him, then he started reading all the great books. He would pick a book if he had seen the movie version and vice versa. And you had the foundation of a quiet, well spoken, talented young man with passion and imagination. He would have gone on to become almost anything he wanted if it were not for his doting mother. She loved him too much. Is it possible for a mother to love a son too much? For Miles Crewes the result was devastating. Instead of an eventful challenging life. Miles was pampered and smothered with kindness. He was brought up without worry and made to feel that he was perfect. The ambition to succeed was contorted to one of simplicity and immature pursuit of pleasure. His main concern in his early life was to feel loved and excel at kindness. It manifested in a total lack of commitment to anything important. Everything was important, he spread joy and happiness and was well liked. But he took no chances. Far be it for him to try something and fail. His mother and then everyone would see that he was not perfect.

He was raised in the small town of Parkes isolated from the real world and the coastline cities teeming with life. He was the brightest and best in a community best described as mediocre.

Parkes would have stayed that way for eternity but they had the Dish; The famous satellite dish that allowed NASA to communicate with Apollo 11 when they landed on the moon. Since then Parkes assumed its place in the space race lore. Myles was just a boy when the town   achieved their 15 minutes of fame.

He was ruggedly handsome and tall. He wore his hair longish to keep up with the trend, but he was not trendy. His mother picked his clothes and shoes until he was 18.
He was always one or two trends behind. His face was round and there were a couple of acne scars. The nose could have been smaller and more roman but his eyes were blue, like the sky and his mother's. Even there she favored him. His sister and brother got the fathers dull brown eyes. He was never overweight but neither was he thin. His body was thick and darker than his siblings. Again his mothers skin, the rest of them fair skinned and thinner.

The only thing his mother did not give him was her light hair. His hair was brown and curly like the men in the family; his sister got the blond curls.

All in all he was a good looking young man. Confident that he could not fail at becoming a fine actor, that was his dream.

But his dream would come to an end one sunny afternoon while he was visiting Newcastle on the coast during a championship rugby match; which his team won handily. And there on the edge of the Tasmian Sea while he walked on the beach he heard a lovely voice calling his name.

When he turned to the voice she came up to him and asked him to sign her book of autographs. He was bewitched by her beauty and flattered by his celebrity.

"You were marvelous   last night...two scores, and against our champion boys."

"We were lucky; your mates are very good"

"Such praises, you are very nice, but you clobbered us good, it wasn't close."

They shared a good smile.

"You know my name but I don't know yours?"

"Michelle Gibson"

His mother had not prepared him for women. He was shy with them and unsure of himself. Back home he attended the parties and school dances but he rarely danced or spoke to the girls. He could not understand why he was so shy. His only girlfriend was a girl who lived next door who he knew from childhood and who used to play with all the boys when they played rugby or soccer and they would all take turns feeling her up. He didn't like it very much but it did not stop him from taking liberties with her. She liked him and told him one day after an especially rowdy game when they walked home and then she asked him to kiss her and when he did, he had a girlfriend. But before they could get around the bases her family moved away and he was left with longing for the comely girl, who his mother said was not good enough for him.

And now here he was face to face with a beautiful woman who was leaving nothing to his imagination.

"Myles would you like to take me to a movie tonight?" She said to him with just the right balance of confidence and flirtation.

"Yea, sure." He managed.

"Ok then, meet me at the Grand Theatre on Bishop Road for the 7 o'clock show." And she leaned over and kissed him lightly on his lips and ran up the sand into the parking lot.

He followed her with his eyes all the way to where she met a group of other girls and after a few minutes of giggling and looking his way got into a car and drove away.

He ran all the way to the team's hotel and borrowed a nice shirt from one of the best dressers and got a ride from one of the coaches to the theatre.

"You need a condom?" he asked him before he got out of the car.

"No, thanks it's not that kind of a date."

"Here take one or two; you never know where you end up on date at your age." The wise coach handed him the two packets.

Myles was now more nervous than before as he thanked him.

He was early and had to wait for her for a few minutes. The movie was "The Road Warrior" with Mel Gibson, he was glad, he had already seen it but it would be great to see it again.

When she arrived in a car driven by another girl she went straight to him and kissed him lightly on the lips like before.

"I was looking forward to seeing you again." She said before he could say it. It would be like that for them, she was always one step ahead of him.

"I love Mel Gibson; he's my cousin you know." She said it

so casually that it really   floored Myles.

"Oh man, that's fantastic, what's he like, do you see him often, are you close?"

She was laughing loudly enjoying his illusion.

"You silly boy, I'm going to have fun with you, you can't be this gullible?"

"Ha, ha...you got me good." He tried to salvage some dignity.

"I'll get you back, you'll see." He said still trying to catch up.

"No you won't, I'm too quick for you." She bounced away and was through the theatre doors before he could say anything else.

It was right after the scene where Gibson is eating dog food that she snuggled up to him, he reached over and put his arm around her. She turned her face and he kissed her. It was a real wet, hungry kiss that lasted till the music changed in the movie with a crescendo.

She casually turned her face and watched the movie again. Myles could not watch the movie anymore. This was a first for him. He could see the same movie through two or three showings and never lose concentration. But now he could not care what was on the screen all he could think about was the warm luscious woman that sat beside him.

When she shifted in her seat he placed the arm that had been around her shoulders on her lap on top of hers and caressed her hand gently. She did not resist him. She did not move her head or body as she pulled her hand from under his and placed it on top of his hand. His hand now lay on her thigh. He was deep in concentration, for the next move was going to be something bold, something new, it would be life-changing. He slowly, very slowly moved his hand between her thighs and ever so gently almost indiscernible began to caress her inner thigh.

He was in a state of ecstasy. He could not look at her, but he was looking at the movie and seeing only her.

She finally shifted a little and he thought about pulling his hand back. But when he made an effort and peeked at her he was amazed to see that her face was pure delight. He did not stop until she put her hand once again on his, not to stop him but to get him to look at her as she leaned towards him and they kissed passionately again.

Afterwards she took him to a local hangout where they met up with her girlfriends and their dates. Throughout the meal he could not keep his hands off her and they shared many more kisses and caresses even in front of her friends.

Almost a Year Later.

> *My Dearest Love:*
> *I write this with trembling hands at the anticipation of making love to you tonight. My heart is full. Full of Michelle. My friend, my lover, my destiny. I remember praying for someone to share my life. God heard me. Even when I doubted my faith. No more. He answered*

my prayers. He   sent me an Angel. And my Angel named Michelle picked me up and whispered, "You are a good man and I believe in you. I give myself to you." Now I have hope, love, and confidence. I owe you this; you have made me a better man. I want to be with you. I want to be there for you! With my newfound strength and the love you have given me, I will be the man you want. I pray for this and God will not forsake me.

I will take the early bus on Friday and be in your arms this Saturday. We both know it is a selfish sacrifice for two people to hide our feelings and actions from our loved ones like this but we deserve these two glorious days in each others embrace. I will be there holding you as I hope and pray to be there for you the rest of our lives. I say these words clearly with conviction and without hesitation, I love you. I will strive to earn your love. I felt it the last time we were together when you told me how much you wanted to be with me. Not the sex or the fame. But just being next to you.

I feel the same. I never felt like this before. It hurts when I leave you. If it were just the two of us we would be together now. But I understand. We will make it work; we will make it to our destinies. And when the time comes, no matter when, I will come to you and whisper, you are the woman of my dreams, I want to spend the rest of our lives together. This is our destiny. Love Myles

Myles read the letter a   several times, making small corrections and additions before sealing it in the envelope and running down to the post office to mail it personally.

They had spent the last few months meeting in Newcastle. He would drive down when he could borrow his father's car or like the last time, he rode the bus.

The first time he had gone back to see her he rented a small room on the beach in a small cheap hotel. They made love. They were both virgins but their lust provided all the knowledge they needed. Within a few months they were veterans. As if lovemaking was always a part of their lives. So natural. So innocent. So satisfying. There was no planning or rules of foreplay. Just pure lust and infatuation. In their innocence they could have been doing the wrong things, but it sure felt right.

And now he would see her in five days time and he counted the hours until he would have her in his arms.

This time it would be different. There would be no lovemaking. There would only be tears and words.

"I'm pregnant"

How could that be? They counted so well to the day, even hours. The rhythm method worked if you counted right. He cursed himself.

Michelle cried and assured him it was not his fault. After all he was perfect. How could he make a mistake like this? He counted the days. It must have been her cycle. He could not have been wrong.

"I should have used a condom!"

They tried in the beginning but it felt awful and they kept tearing. He said he would count the days. She said she wanted him like nature intended without any messy condoms. And now as nature intended she was bringing forth life. The will of God. The miracle of birth to procreate mankind.

They held each other and swore allegiance to their love. They would get married. Begin their lives together. Count their blessings and go forth confidently in love.

After careful planning they would elope the next month and go live in Sydney to the south. They would find work and raise their family. They talked about an abortion. But she had cried. They would decide in Sydney, but she would convince him to have the baby, she could talk him into anything.

Michelle closed her bank accounts and with some of the money they bought a used car. They piled it full of her things that she could sneak out of her house, his things they would get later when they were married. He borrowed some money from one of his coaches and they started for Sydney early in the morning while it was still dark. Just outside Newcastle, a mere 50 miles into their trip. A tired, overworked driver of a big eighteen wheeler, lost control of his rig. Myles swerved to avoid the collision but he could not turn fast enough. The small compact in which they were riding was hit with tremendous force and sent hurling, rolling over several times. When the car landed, incredibly right-side up on its wheels, Myles was dazed and there was a gaping wound over his left eye, but he was conscious. He looked next to him and Michelle was not there. He tried to open the door but it was jammed shut. He crawled out of the window and ran back to the scene of the accident. On the shoulder of the road was a woman leaning over a body. She was cradling her head softly praying.

"...give us this day our daily bread; and forgive us our trespasses as we forgive those who trespass against us, and lead us not into temptation; but deliver us from evil. Amen."

Miles knelt down beside her and looked at the lifeless face of his beloved Michelle. She had been tossed from the car breaking her neck, killing her and their baby instantly.

When he heard his voice say Amen, he began to cry uncontrollably.

"Why couldn't you take me? Why couldn't you take me!!!?"

The sobs turned to anger and rage as he repeated his plea.

He knew at last that he was not perfect.

23

Newcastle, Australia 1986

He was still numb. His soul was empty. He didn't know what to do about anything. Somehow he kept functioning. He was cynical about everything, and a hard edge began to form around his persona. He blamed himself. His mother comforted him in the only way she could, with love and kindness.

For the very first time he could not respond. He resented her and avoided her when he could. He did not need love or kindness. All he wanted was judgment and guilt. This pain, this loss would be his destiny. He would mourn Michelle forever.

When his mind allowed his soul to function, he began to dream again. But they were temporary fixes. He knew the time to act was near. He felt he must awake into action or forever languish in self-pity and his mother's perfect world. At times he thought he had a chance. He could anticipate a spark that would ignite the flames; the juices would flow and out would come an idea. But then to put those ideas into action, that was the question. To find the solution in him, now that was his dilemma.

For the very first time in his life he was not special in some way. He had always felt that everyone has something special in them. Every living thing in this world has the instincts, feelings and soul to feel their own uniqueness and individuality. That is what makes us and this existence worthwhile. When we lose that special feeling, we are doomed to depression, despair and mediocrity. He had always hoped and prayed that never happened to him.

Every once in a while he pictured himself in heaven with Michelle. It was bliss. But soon he was engulfed in flames.

"I was wrong! I have been wrong!" He lamented.

He craved to be punished. To suffer for his having survived. His wish would be granted within months.

A Few Months Later.

Louis Franklin was already too old to play rugby when he talked his way into the Newcastle Rugby team. It was his dream to play for his hometown club. He had little talent but he made up for it with ambition and speed for a man his age. So he made the team and was the leading scorer. He was an overachiever.

He would play the match with vigor and an uncanny will to win, making long runs and artful passes with his trademark catchphrase "Oh Jesus!" at almost predictable intervals.

"OH, Jesus" was a sigh that was half-audible, a resigned acceptance to his faith.

The "Oh, Jesus" that cut through the huddled bodies hurled together after a brutal tackle by the star player of the opposing team the one they called the "The Tasmanian Devil", Myles Crewes, bore no resemblance to a sigh. It was shriek of anguish, unsuccessfully muffled, such a piteous cry for help. It startled the rough and toughest of these men that play this most violent of sports. Louis would never play the game nor would he walk. He was paralyzed instantly from the waist down after his spinal cord was snapped by the brute force of Myles' blow.

Several years later.

Myles lived in Newcastle in one of those seedy hotels that line the downtown streets, in a warm, damp room with a whirring ceiling fan marking time. He lived with an aborigine woman he called Mattie short for the Matilda in the song. Her real name was Yunupingu and she once was active and well known in the native rights movement until a man broke her heart and spirit and she gave up on life. She lay naked on the dirty sheets. The fat black woman, who had seen much more of the animal side of life than Myles could ever imagine, was his sole contact with humanity. He had met her in one of his acting gigs, for he was acting, finally. Very small parts in those violent pessimistic small budget movies that had made Mel Gibson famous like The Road Warrior when he met Michelle. He was always offered the most violent parts. The sadistic killer. After all he was the only athlete banned from Rugby for violent play. But he was an actor at last.

Mattie had taken him in and gave him a home and took care of him, on and off for the past few years.

In this unholy room he would think of Michelle and what could have been. He began to think about joining her. The depression snuck up on him. The bouts of despair followed by heavy drinking and violence toward the black woman. Then the tears. Tears over the most insignificant stuff, they would come uncontrollably without reproach over a scene in a movie he had seen many times or after he beat the living crap-out of Mattie.

His mind reeling from   loneliness, despair, and guilt, the scene would touch a nerve and the deluge came.

He would sometimes cry just sitting in his favorite overstuffed chair after evoking a thought of Michele or of Louis.

The aborigine would laugh at him sometimes, begging for a beating. He would oblige with quick slap or kick, anything to humiliate her.

At night, sleep was an adventure. He could no longer distinguish the dreams from the nightmares. They seemed to blend together. One moment he was playing rugby, swimming or laughing with fellow actors, the next he was fighting for his life on some alleyway where cats or dogs would spring from under his feet, his nerves tested to the limit by bullets flying around him, until he was hit or cut with knife. He could feel the heat from the wound; feel his body on fire drain the precious blood. And at the time of death he would always awake, usually in a cold sweat. He would look at the black woman and wonder how she managed to sleep so soundly. He despised her.

An athlete knows that exercise can clear your head and settle your nerves so he pushed himself. He arose early from bed and ran to the beach where he ran on the shore until he could not take another step. He then swam out far from shore. Everyday a little farther out to Sea. Thoughts of swimming out until he could no longer swim goaded his frail mind.

The aborigine became a familiar sight, sitting on the coarse sands of Newcastle Beach, while on her lap she played with some stones. Never taking her eyes off the man who ran in the shore or swam in the   ocean.

Then one morning as he stood calmly by the water's edge and waited until that inner voice would come and speak to him with soft words like a siren's song and temp him to make his last swim he heard another voice.

"Myles...Myles! Oh Jesus! MYLES!!!"

He turned and saw the man in the wheelchair waving at him. Louis Franklin used his arms to beckon Myles to come to him. Myles could not recognize Louis but the voices went silent. He moved toward the other voice, a familiar one that was calling his name. Mattie watched them from a distance.

"Myles, It's been a while, how have you been mate?"

"Life's a bitch, but I guess you know that"

"Well she can be."

"Is that your Sheila?" Louis asked him as he looked beyond him to the black figure sitting in the sand.

"She's nobody."

"Myles I have thought of you a lot these last few months."

"Lucky you, I've tried to forget you, but it's no good. I guess you know what I mean."

The crippled man nodded.

"Myles I have been following your career and I tracked you down, I need a favor?"

"So you are a fan of fine acting".

They both smiled.

"Well a man has to do what the Lord asks of him, and I guess you haven't been listening. I think you are better than the roles you've played."

"It is the only roles I am good for"

"Why in God's name would you think that?"

"Just look in the goddamn mirror, you are one of my finest achievements!"

"Is that what you really feel deep down in your heart, Myles"?

"Louis everything I touch turns to shit. I'm good for nothing." *This world is better off without me*; he wanted to add but held back.

"Myles I need your help with a project I am heading, will you at least listen to what I have to say?"

"What could you possibly want with the likes of me?"

"OH Jesus man, stop with all the self-pitying crap and listen to me!"

"Well I guess I owe you at least that much." Myles said sarcastically running his hand over the wheel of the crippled man's chair.

Louis reached out with his muscular arms and grabbed Myles's right arm and brought him down forcefully to his knees next to the wheelchair. Myles did not resist. Louis looked into his eyes and saw it all. Surrender, despair there was nothing left in the empty shell.

"You don't owe me shit!"

Myles face contorted trying to hold back the tears. But this was the right time. Here was the moment that he had been waiting for. That moment when all those tearful sessions he had endured, prepared him, like a   well-rehearsed scene, for at this moment he put his arms around the crippled man and let the genuine tears flow with their accompanying sobs. It lasted a few minutes.

"It's all right my son, it's all right, go ahead and let it out, it's all right"

After a while when he could speak he spoke softly from his heart.

"I am sorry Louis, can you ever forgive me?"

"Yes, mate I forgive you, I forgave you the day after it happened in the Hospital when you came to visit me. But I realize you didn't want to be forgiven then. The time was not right. You had to put yourself through your own bloody hell for you to end up here. And now, the question is; are you ready to forgive yourself?"

"I don't know if I can, I'm empty, there is nothing left".

"Then come with me and I will help you find something to fill you up."

"I don't know, I don't know".

Louis opened his jacket and Myles saw the priest's collar.

"Myles the day I sat in this wheelchair was the beginning of the rest of my life. I realized very quickly why God chose this for me. I was wandering and had too many distractions in my life. I always wanted to do the Lord's work, and only when I sat in this chair was I ready to give my life to him. I thank you for your hand in this. I am going to be ordained next month and I want you to come."

All Myles could do was   nod his head and lean it against the shoulder of the man he had despised too long and who he blamed for all his pain.

The sun rose brilliantly and they both watched it for a while this way.

And the aborigine Yunupingu began to walk on the shore towards the sunrise, never looking back, never to be seen by Myles again.

23

The Village of Teruan, Colombia 1999

Fr. Myles Crewes was dreaming as he slept on a straw mat on the floor of the rustic one room cabin in the Village of Teruan. He was dreaming about dolphins, the ones with the tusks like Unicorns. They were under the floor where he slept enclosed in glass. Everyone knew they were there except him. He finally reached out and petted a baby one and felt hair not fish. Beautiful eyes looked back at him. He wanted to free them. There were questions as to how long they had been there. Never mind how they got there. Overall it was a happy but strange dream. He was awake and it was gone.

It was the middle of November already! Where had all the time gone! "Yeah, I know!" he said to himself. It has gone into the marrow of my bones where it hung around until he felt the sharp claws of the demons that toyed with his soul. And just when he thought they had him...he fought back. He came alive again as if he had been in a deep sleep in some dark place.

The birds were singing outside, he could see them through the window. For a minute it reminded him of the other window so many years ago it seemed, the one where he could see Louis feeding his birds the left-over biscuits and bread.

There was so much of his sinful past that he had erased from his memory. Some of it seemed like a bad dream. But it had happened and he survived and now he was here living a life he never imagined.

Meeting Louis that day on the beach in Newcastle was divine intervention. From that moment forward he began a new life. A life that would take him on a long journey of discovery and salvation that would change him forever.

He was so close to ending his life that day. God had other plans for him. He was finally at peace with who he was and what he was to do on this earth to fulfill his destiny.

The day he attended Louis's ordination was the first day of his new life. As he watched a man who he thought he had crushed, a cripple, half a man to many, and there he was alive and bigger than life, jubilant and with more hope and faith than anyone he had known. Myles came face to face with the power of redemption. He did not turn away or ignore the moment; he seized it, wrapped his muscular arms around it and held on for dear life. He had no idea why, all he knew is that if he ever let go his life would end.

He stood in the front pew of the seminary, as he always did; not hiding behind but out in front where everyone could see him there was nothing holding him back. He was not acting he was living. He was tired of the half-truths the outright lies and the despair. He wanted more not less. His conversion had gone without fanfare or any material rewards, his conversion had been within. Inside his heart. He saw everything with new eyes of faith. As he stood in the front pew he noticed that it was Good Friday's mass, it was different, there were no rituals. A priest read from the gospel. He listened. The Stations of the Cross. Christ carrying his cross. To his left a big heavy cross appeared. It was carried by some aborigines, he thought he saw Mattie. They carried the cross around the entire floor of the church. As the reader read each station. They moved. He felt the pain. He was humbled. Right then and there he was one with the man carrying the cross. There was an overwhelming feeling of regret, to save him, the arrogance; he was only doing what he was set on earth to do. He was so grateful. He finally understood the sacrifice. He did not know why but he walked up to the altar and said thank you, thank you, thank you, and he laid on the floor his arms outstretched, humbled, he could not get any lower...thank you, thank you, was all he said.

He followed Louis into the priesthood. His calling was not instantaneous, but it was sure and true. His new friend was his guide then his mentor and now his inspiration. Louis died of an infectious fever that previous winter. His last words to Myles; "My brother I love you, thank you, I am proud of you, finish our work... God Bless You."

Father Myles Crewes accepted the poorest parish on the South American continent in the highlands of Colombia. A dangerous and violent area sorely needing to hear the word of God. Thank God he was the best student in his Spanish class back in Parkes. He always wondered why he took that class in a language that he would never use. He knew now.

He would preach from his small church on Sundays to a small congregation in the Village of Teruan about a hundred miles from the small town of Puerto Narino. On weekdays he ventured into the jungle and nearby hills to preach to the remote villages and towns that had no church.

"Padre Cruz" they called him. It translated to "Father Cross" but it was just the mistaken pronunciation of his difficult last name. When someone explained this to him, his eyes welled up; he told them he was not worthy.

Alexander, Illapa & Myles

"In the middle of difficulty lies opportunity."
-Albert Einstein

24

Village of Teruan, Colombia Easter 2000

Alex and Illapa were going to meet the Priest. Dominique had told them not to leave until they spoke to him.

They had gotten off the main path heading out of the village. They wanted to drink from a nearby stream with pristine water running through a bluff of trees, too small to call a forest, but enchanting and beckoning. They both stood drinking not the water but the beauty of the glen just long enough to feel special, to once again don the rose colored glasses and pausing, gaping, browsing, through a world of colored canvasses propped up on the walls and fences of trees   that hemmed the glen. They drank in the beauty of the people in the canvasses. The ones in the village and the ones making their way to the bluff.

They were not like them, for they belonged to this place. Natural, exotic, strange yet familiar to them somehow. Alex and Illapa were different and they were missing out.

They felt like tourists again. It was a voice that lured them from the array of canvasses. Impelled towards the sound they moved among the people and made their way to the inner circle of a clearing in the woods. Across from them stood figure moving slowly through a group of people. On every side of the clearing there were people. Raptly following the figure absorbing his words.

She and Alex moved among them until magically, they were sitting on the low end of the clearing on a soft patch of green. Beside them a group from the village that they recognized as the elders welcomed them with soft smiles. They began to chant, their voices soft and mellow. Alex and Illapa looked up and saw the blue sky, and they sat, still under the spell, enchanted, until driven by the magic they opened the ears of their hearts and heard HIS voice for the first time.

"From the time we are children we are told to love one another, by our parents first, then by the priests, yet we do not listen. This is a question that I have asked myself many times. Why can't we love one another?. The answer lies in our hearts. We listen with our ears and our minds. And judge first. We then run what we hear through our life's filters with all our prejudices, fears, doubts and pain. Then we act.

But our actions are compromised   by our sins. It is only when we open our hearts to our Lord and listen with our hearts that we can act with his goodness and find true love. Unless you receive his gift left for all of us to share you cannot call yourselves children of God. For when you receive his Holy Spirit you will see change in you. An irreversible change for the good. First you then everyone you touch will see and feel the presence of God in you. Then and only then can you call yourself a child of God."

He moved all around his flock. A knowing glance, a gentle touch and his essence was peace and love.

"For we are all God's children on earth. we are going to be fine. He will feed you when you are hungry. Clothe you when you are naked. And comfort you when you are treated cruelly by your enemies. We are always under his care. Rejoice with me, teach your children, sing your songs, tell your stories. Always know that he is with you. And most of all, love one another with passion and integrity. You are all better today, this moment because of what you have endured. He has always been with us. It was his hand that helped you plant your crops and feed your children. It was his words that reconciled you with your loved ones and with your enemies. It was his power and strength that helped you survive and bring you here. And here is where we will pray with our brothers and sisters. Your ancestors are here also with us. We are here to forgive and love one another. The flesh and the spirit are all here with us right now. Their holy voices cry out to us through our beloved savior. Love one another as he loves us! Love your children, teach them. Reach out and do the Lord's work. Pray. He will always answer you. All that you ask in his holy name will be granted to you. Because you asked and had the courage and strength to seek him. Through him all

things are possible. Amen"

Voices sang a hymn with passion. The priest leading the voices. It was an ancient dialect. But the melody was familiar. Amazing Grace.

It was a mass of sorts, at the end of the song the people began to move about the clearing and although the sermon was over his words were alive in the words and faces of the people.

She and Alex talked with some of the people they knew. One of Paco's young sons came over and sat on Illapa's lap. After a short while Paco and the priest came over to Alex and the princess and sat on the grass with them. On his lap he opened a very old Bible and began to read in silence.

It was strange for him to hear his name pronounced perfectly in the clearing that strange morning. He moved towards them because he had been told that there were two dangerous criminals hiding in the next Village, a man and woman. They had been there for days keeping to themselves but walking around the village and the people. They had to be criminals because only criminals or scientists dare to venture so far into the jungle. And they did not have any instruments. In fact they were without many possessions and needed food and clothing for which they paid handsomely. But they were not violent and showed affection to each other and the villagers.

It was not easy for them. It took Alex a long time before he began to talk.

"Father, bless me for I have sinned. It has been far too long since I believed in God much less confessed my sins. But I need to talk to someone who could   make sense of my life; they say you are a good man, a good priest who understands suffering and sin."

"Go On my Son" Myles thought of stopping him and asking for some privacy from the beautiful Indian woman beside him holding his hand. But something in the way she looked at him made him comfortable. He sensed she knew everything the young man was about to say.

"I don't know where to begin its been so long, I've been so far from God, perhaps I've gone too far, I don't know if it's too late for me. I've doubted and denied him for so long."

"Don't worry son, just go on and say what you need to tell him, please go on."

"Father my sins are so great, I feel that there's no hope for me. But I want there to be hope. I've been so wrong, so angry…but I don't want to hate anymore. I have no hate left in me. Here in the mountains I feel the closest I've ever felt to God. And yet I cannot forget the pain, the hate for those that hurt me and my family. I've killed men and lusted for revenge. In the end it gave me no release, just more pain. I want to stop running. I want to love this woman who is so much like me. But I fear it may be too late for us. Can God forgive us and our past lives? And give us new ones?"

"My son tell me about your life, let God know your sins and he will soothe your pain, go on my son."

"Father I wanted to rape a woman a wife of a man that that hurt me, I terrorized them, I committed acts of terrorism, I bombed a ship killing innocent men and women, I had sex with women I did not love, I lied to women and men, and I took the Lord's name in vain and denied his existence. I do not deserve his mercy. Father can God forgive my sins?"

It took Alex almost a half an hour to say everything he needed to say. When he finished he thought he had only spoken for a few minutes.

"My son your sins are great and your suffering has served its purpose. You must pray every day at least five minutes for the lives of the men and women that you have injured and for all of those that lost their lives because of your actions. You must find a way to make peace with them and ease their suffering. It will not be easy. But you will have no peace until you do this. I will help you. May the Almighty God have mercy on you, and forgiving your sins, bring you life everlasting. Amen."

Then he lifted his right hand and traced a cross on Alex's forehead. "May the Almighty and Merciful God grant you pardon, absolution, and remission of your sins".

And then the Princess spoke and confessed to him in Spanish and when she was finished, the sun was high in the blue sky, a calm breeze reached them and they felt the presence of the universe and a force inside them raised their spirits. They both felt good, it had been a long time since they felt like this, good and safe.

Linda

"A man who was completely innocent, offered himself as a sacrifice for the good of others, including his enemies, and became the ransom of the world. It was a perfect act."
                    Mohandas Gandhi

25

Miami, Florida 1998

Linda Russo-Garcia, that was her name now. Still using her late husband's name out of respect. For that is what everyone thought. Alex committed suicide like his mother. Only his body had never been found. But Linda knew the truth.

She was a gorgeous creature. A model's figure that pulled attention to the mournful eyes, still the loveliest blue, exciting and expressive, mirroring the very soul of their owner.

She had loved once, and once was enough. Somehow Linda had become a heartbreaker, taking from men who offered her their whole lives only their sympathy, their time, their warmness, but never giving her love, which she locked up again waiting for the healing of the still-fresh wounds. Of what could have been. Then, when she   had come through friendship to find love again, she found she had more to give. But she always wondered whether it was the real thing. She found how to give, not in passion but in tenderness, not just her body but her thoughts, her life, and the future loomed ahead with a promise that soon she would be completely cleansed. One night Linda decided to get totally drunk because she had never done it before. Her new love was out of town, she was with friend, a loose girl but well-meaning one who left Linda, bottle-in-hand sitting on a bed in the care of another friend, a man that Linda's friend trusted and whom she admonished as she left, "Take good care of Linda, I'll be back in an hour." And in an hour, Linda lost life and hope and love. She went back to work the next day, trying to forget, knowing only that her friend had returned to find her asleep and the man gone, never to be heard of again. Two months later, the fact of pregnancy confronted Linda. To tell the man she loved would be to break his heart, to break all the trust he had put in her. It was such a needless crime, such a horrible trick of fates, played on the beautiful woman who had been through so much. To suffer the very depths of despair again, to want to die so badly and so strongly that she sometimes resorted to physical violence to unleash some of her fury, to plunge from the very summit of all that was good and noble to the hell in which she found herself was too much for her to reveal. She left the beloved, and, because he was the only thing in the world that mattered to her, she tried to soften the blow and invented a trip with her family to put distance between them.

Whatever spiritual conscience that plagued her after her ordeal dictated now, that this would be a wretched and miserable life to bring forth. The child would be killed. She would not take the risk, the judgments and isolation. She made the wrong decision. But at the very least she now had a new perception of Alex's loss. For the very first time she began to understand him.

Downtown Miami a Few Days Later.

Linda Russo-Garcia was still the raving beauty that she always thought she was. Her looks and grit had helped her get to where she was today. She felt that she could have reached a higher position at FBI but for a pretty face and her sex barred her from getting the job she deserved. She knew very few at the Bureau headquarters in D.C., no one knew where she was and her assumption that Miami would be her worst refuge proved wrong as weeks and months went by without incident. Every now and then she would run into some of her co-workers who laughed and just seemed to know how to be just enough condescending or patronizing or trying hard to be "nice" to the beautiful woman whose ex-husband was on their list of most wanted criminals. Yet she always held her own. Magically holding a veil of sorrow across her eyes; the lips would smile and sometimes even laugh with them and the voice would be gay for a while but the eyes...the eyes never lost their sorrow, their longing for something which no one could understand. Only

Mark, her father understood   and she marveled at the depth of love he had for her. In Linda's mind her father had been touched by God to command such devotion. Yes, it was possible he could forgive Alex. She often wished she could.

It was business as usual in downtown Miami on a Monday in November. It was cool but no hint of a real winter.

Linda was handed a confidential folder.

Afterwards she leaned back on her leather chair, and looking out the window at the water in Biscayne Bay opened the file and began to read. Her pulse quickened and her jaw tensed. All caused by the words she had just read. The pictures were not clear and she could barely make out the faces but she knew. A wife always knows.

Alex and a woman were holding hands in the midst of a tribal meeting or Village gathering. A man was speaking to the group with a book in his hand. The red circles around her ex-husband and the woman made her look closer with a magnifying glass. She was not looking at Alex but the sharper much better image of the beautiful exotic Indian woman next to him.

It had been seven years since she had last seen a picture of him. She was briefed that he was alive but that his whereabouts were unknown. He was however out of favor with the PRC.

The last entry in his folder said that he was disillusioned with the PRC and that he had gone into hiding somewhere in South America. The FBI and Interpol had classified his status as an inactive terrorist.

Linda placed his file on the desk and looked out of her

window for a few minutes.   She then reached for the file titled; ***Illapa. Shinning path operative and terrorist.***

She read every scrap of paper and studied all the pictures. There was not much in the file. But she took it all in. In the end she said softly.

"A perfect match."

She spoke into the phone to her secretary.

"Maggie, I need you book me a trip to Washington for tomorrow. I am going home early to pack. Have the ticket sent to my apartment."

Linda was thinking ahead.

She reached into her personal folders and pulled out an old document and began to read it once more.

My Dearest Linda:

Please do not think for a moment that I leave you because we fight and argue. I leave you because I am dead inside. I leave because I can only cause you more pain. It is my own salvation that I seek, a goal or purpose to this life I have been born to. Do not cry for me. Please remember me for sacrificing myself to your own happiness. I couldn't care less about anything else in this world but that you find happiness somewhere with someone that deserves your love. Hate me if you wish if it helps you cope and give you a reason that will make sense in your world. But I will never hate you or forget you. You will always be my saving grace from my old life. It is you I will miss. Nothing else. They are all gone. It is over for me.

With all my love.

Alex.

But now was the time. She would make them understand

and she would use all her   power and skills to get them to agree to send her to bring back Alex to face Justice.

But she wondered if she was doing it for Justice or for Vengeance. It would take her a few days of contemplation to tell her father about her mission.

A Few Weeks Later.

"What a wonderful day to be alive!" She was exulting in the fresh breeze that was throwing sea-foam into the boat. It was a Morgan Out-Island 41 ketch. A nice present to a daughter for her graduation from law school.

She was going to need a little alcohol and plenty of distractions when she unloaded on her father. It would take all her courage. She really had no idea if he would object on the dangerous grounds or what she flatly expected; why YOU!

Mark had eased into the noveau riche society of Miami, and now in this futile attempt to fit-in he wanted his daughter to join him. The Morgan was old but in good shape, the better yachts were moored in Dinner Key also, and they were bigger and newer, the real wealth, and she knew her way around them, the new boat was a first step. It was not easy getting close to the owners of those other boats. There was a time when nothing had been easy for her. She had studied hard to graduate at the top of her class. She had fought, made a fool of herself for this chance to come to rub elbows with the elite of Miami, and it had been months now since her entrance into the Yacht Club ceased to turn the heads of the members.

You meet three kinds of people at the Yacht Club. The old money, the new, and all the rest of the local natives and "wanna-be's" picking up the latest fad to take up their idle time. The first two groups she cultivated and the last group would follow, they always followed the other two. So she mingled and moved confidently among them, and finally here she was, the first woman to lead an FBI district office, still far from her goal, but satisfying nevertheless.

"Man, what a life, Dad, you can just set that right here and bring me some more limes—I want to match this glass to the green of the sea." Mark would oblige-he was her favorite waiter. All she had to do was sit there and sort of hold court—indulge, you know? Her brothers were skin-diving; their friends, a young couple who had driven up with them were down below, probably getting in a quickie before lunch. Linda and Mark who kept appearing with more tall glasses full of scotch and rum and ice and whatever bubbly soda there was, and now she was going to match the drink to the color of the ocean. She'd match it to the palm tree fronds that swung out over the shoreline only a short distance from the anchored boat but that would take too much lime and then she wouldn't be able to drink the stuff. Linda's hands were slender; the fingers ended in long, perfectly polished nails, one of her private joys. She bent, reaching for a lime and the uncombed tangle that was once bangs fell forward, creating a sudden shade for the squinting eyes. Linda never got roaring drunk anymore, she was touchy about it for obvious reasons; but

the taste of liquor pleased her   still and she would sit for
hours, letting amounts of alcohol that would wipe out a lesser
person settle through her system, with only one noticeable effect;
a faint smile simply stayed on her face matching the languid
poses into which she'd throw the almost-skinny body. But
nowadays she knew when to stop; she controlled her alcohol,
like everything else in her new life, with precision and will.

Very slowly, very meticulously, she cut through one lime
and then another, measuring the fullest part of the green sphere
and cutting gently all the way to the other side. After squeezing
each half into the glass she put it close to the water, leaning back,
calculating the precise intensity of green beyond the foam. It took
one and a half limes to perfect the drink. Linda stretched the
long, lean legs, one arm went over the side, fingers dipped in the
restless water, one arm curved, elbow resting on the table, slowly
bringing the glass to her lips, then letting the stuff drip down
into her throat while the breeze flicked back her hair, bringing
the squint back to her eyes.

"Hey Linda, want to come see the cave they were talking
about? Hey Linda, you lazy slob, come on and do some nature
appreciation..."

"Go to hell", but she was too languid to say it out loud.
The brothers gave up. That was a good thing about these
people—you did whatever the hell you pleased and nobody
questioned your motives. So, she'd show them nature
appreciation when they finally came on board.

"Hey, see that-how can you tell without smelling that I

haven't got sea-water right here in this glass. Is that nature appreciation or not?" Yeah, but she wouldn't say it in so many words—she'd just hold up the glass near the water and point. If they didn't get it like that, forget it.

Mark came back out; she said "Food!" By late afternoon Linda was crying. That was how it used to be whenever she had a moment alone, she'd start thinking and remembering. About Alex and about her life.

"Linda what's wrong you haven't tied one on like this in a long time, what's eating you?" Mark tried to hold her hand but she pulled it away.

"You better have another drink, because this one is going to floor you!" She looked at him with bloodshot eyes.

"I'm going after Alex, we know where he is hiding with his terrorist whore." She tried not to show the hurt in her eyes. "I'm going to bring him to face justice and ME!" She said avoiding his eyes.

"I'm going after him, I wanted you to know, no need to tell you it's my ass if this gets out."

"Geez! Yeah I bet!" he said.

"Dad I know you must have been his contact with the Govt. his dossier alludes to his attempts to justify his actions."

She handed her father the file.

"I don't want to know anything, I just want you to understand." She finished still avoiding his eyes.

"Before you go I need to tell you a few things." Mark just looked at her with reassuring, loving father's gaze.

Mark told her about   Alex's timely phone calls to him and his part in helping him escape.

"I'm glad it's you, for you are the only one that can save him." He said as he hugged his daughter and held her as she cried softly in his arms.

Alex, Illapa, Fr. Myles & Linda

"And all things whatsoever ye shall ask in prayer, believing, ye shall receive."

Jesus Christ (Mark 21:22)

26

The Village of Teruan, Colombia 2000

It was a perfectly wasted weekend. Alex and Illapa feared venturing out as they had heard that some military scouts were in the area. They were afraid again. Why? They felt despair, again. Why? They did not trust their awareness. It was a constant challenge to keep true to their newfound faith. They clamored for that clear voice that spoke the truth, so strong. *A love so true.* They hoped that all resentment and ill will would soon be a distant memory.

"And this too shall pass away". "Ye are Gods." Jesus said.

Now their one true faith sustained them, but was it enough? A man's faith will sustain him above all else. It is more powerful, than love, family, success and hate. It is all consuming and all forgiving. The belief in eternal salvation is the world's promise from God that all will be made new in the end. It was free. Anyone could enjoy this gift. The price was faith.

Blind faith. That search for eternal salvation and glory. Those fortunate to search and find it here on our glorious planet, in the Sea, in the mountains, or lakes, in the forests and desserts are truly blessed. Wherever you plant your seed it will grow with faith. The more time passed the more things began to change for them, their feelings and fears, they got clearer, and some just faded away.

Fr. Myles had told them that on earth humans spend their lives searching for one's other half, even if that search is fruitless, what we don't understand is that ultimately everyone of us will be joined together in the spiritual realm.

He explained that men and women had clung to the saying, "That which God has joined together, let no man put asunder." According to him this reference to marriage is misinterpreted by many. They don't differentiate the civil or religious ceremony with the spiritual union forged by God and in which many marriages or unions may or may not be present. Thus he said, I am not in any means condoning divorce which is simply another human convenience, no he was simply stating that our benevolent God tells us that no matter what happens in our physical life, a true union under God cannot end, it is eternal as the Sun and Moon and   Stars in the Sky.

They were encouraged with his words, for both feared that their choices in partners in the past would always haunt them. But to know that even if their destinies separated them, it was reassuring to know that other perfect half would be waiting. Even if earth failed them, no power on earth could separate them from their love.

Weeks Later.

He had to write it down. Alex sat outside their hut and used a makeshift desk out of an old crate. He looked at the jungle and while he stared he saw the old house again. It was just as if he was a child again. He could see the old woman who argued with all the neighbors who lived next door watering her vegetables with an old black hose. She was wearing the same red dress with the apron and the kerchief tied around her head like Aunt Jemima. And then beyond he saw their beach. The tide was low and the shallows reflected the dying sun between the beach and the pier just to the right. The sea is my poem he thought. "A thousand mirrors each reflecting your indifference..." he said in a soft tone. He remembered his father's poem. The first words came like a whisper.

Here I am in paradise again, one more step toward the dream. And what is the dream? To be free again. To Love again. To take care of her. To write my poem in the mountains and live it. Today is the first day of the rest of my life. I know it's an overused cliché. But it is the first day of my new life. God you *are my new life. Thank you for* *my faith. Thank you for her. Thank you for him.*

He wrote freely for over an hour. Random thoughts and words they were vital, he had to write them down. They were written for him and for her and for the simple joy of documenting the change that was taking place within his soul. And he wanted to make sure that somewhere in plain language and black and white would be a manifest of his feelings. He could come back and read and cherish these thoughts he was having. He went on until the very end. And then his thoughts turned black as he remembered Manny. He fought the memory but it overwhelmed his rational thoughts.

So he wrote it down as best he could.

The moon was low in the night sky. After the blaze of flames it was suddenly very dark. But as he looked at the same place he had written about their beach. He saw a beautiful reflection on the water. No golden sunlight this was moonlight but the same thousand mirrors turned grey and white with shadows in the black of night. It was very different but also very beautiful. What was it my father wrote? "The sun's rays reflected on the sea in the early morning created a golden highway to somewhere better, somewhere new, somewhere free…"

My moon vision in the dark is also taking me somewhere new, better and free.

By the time he finished. Illapa had also finished reading his words. She laid the pages down and leaned across and rested her head on his shoulders and they both looked out at the jungle.

A Few Minutes Later.

Father Myles Crewes was moving quickly through the jungle path his mind racing ahead calculating and finding the right words to use when he faced them. It wasn't far from where the jeep had dropped him off. Thank God for the good man who had alerted him. Some in the Village did not like the new strangers at first. But after Padre Cruz converted them they saw them in their new light. A light he feared would be extinguished by the army captain and soldiers and the gringos that had come with them to his village asking questions about the couple hiding in the jungle. Several of them ran to their priest and they took off immediately.

And there in the village they had just left in the simple office of the rectory Special Agent in Charge Linda Russo-Garcia sat in the darkened room that had the shades rolled shutting out the sun. The weight of the world was on the soft round shoulders that heaved softly beneath the kaki army jacket. Capt. Alvarez left her side and returned with a glass of water. He normally wasn't so bold as to be forward to this American woman, but she was so ravishingly beautiful that he wanted to make an impression.

It was a half-hour before Linda could gather her bearings in the heat and move outside. The untouched glass of water remained where the captain had placed it.

The Captain dared do no more and, when he saw that the

woman had recovered, decided to leave and regroup with his men to await orders.

Linda knew no one up here, no one knew where she was and her assumption that Miami would track her proved wrong as it had been hours since she last heard from them on the Satellite Phone.

Linda had never been in the field before this assignment. She sold it to D.C. with the condition she would be in charge. She was never going to get the job until strings were pulled.

And Mark had pulled them for her. Her father hinted that he had an ace up his sleeve.

She took to the jungle well; her stamina was the only drawback. She should have done more running on the beach back home. But she was here and very close to her prey. She had brought a special team with her. All army trained in anti-terrorist warfare and strategy. The only problem was she was not one of them. They followed her reluctantly and with certain disdain. They amused themselves by cracking blonde jokes and laughing loud enough for her to hear them. Yet when the boss lady held a meeting with that cool demeanor and veil of sorrow across her eyes, they were compelled to follow her lead. Her laugh and voice would be jovial for a while but the eyes, yes they saw it in her eyes, they never lost their sorrow, their longing for something which they could not understand. Only Linda understood and marveled at the depth of feelings she still held for a man who, to the men and women she led, was just a bloodthirsty terrorist.

No, Linda would not   tell them. Yes, it was possible he could have changed and she would forgive him. These thoughts plagued on her lucid moments when she could be calm and look at pros and cons and consider her tragedy almost objectively. There were other times when Linda learned better than to try and open up. She had to trust her crew; she never considered consulting with Capt. Alvarez. This was her operation, guarding her secret and finding Alex before anything could happen to him. Mark had told her to make sure no one harmed him, that is was in the interest of the United States that he not be harmed. Mark had never spoken to her like this. She asked him what he was not telling her. He had looked into her eyes and held her as he told her that she had to cut him some slack. He could not divulge anything else, but his silence spoke volumes. Alex was involved in something with the US government. Perhaps a double agent. This was not the time to ponder such lofty questions. She had one or two questions of her own for him. She wanted him in one piece all to herself for just a few minutes, and then they could tear him to pieces for all she cared.

Minutes Later.

Fr. Myles reached their hut ahead of Paco and stopped when he saw them. Her head resting on his shoulder. There was something about how the two of them almost blended into the jungle vista beyond. Myles caught his breath and gently walked over to them.

"My children how are you today?"

"Father!" The girl uttered in sheer pleasure.

"So good to see you father" Alex chimed in.

"My friends I have come to warn you of danger."

"What is it father?"

"The army is in our Village."

"We will hide until they leave like before." Alex spoke to the priest but the look on the priest's face did not change demeanor.

"Not this time Alex, there are American soldiers with them, and they are looking for you two specifically."

"But how…?"

"I don't know why Alex, I think you won't stand a chance running. I thought about it and I feel that both of you should come to my church where I will give you sanctuary until they leave or until we can plan a safe passage out of danger. Take only what you can carry. We haven't a second to spare."

"Vamonos, ya!" The girl said pulling Alex's arm "Leave everything!"

"No, I will take my notes and writing only."

He came back from the hut with a burlap sack with a rope strap which he slung across his shoulders.

Paco led the way with the priest close behind. Alex and the Illapa kept pace behind them.

"Padre, I think we should take the forest road, it will be a bit longer but we can be sure they will not be on it, as it is hard on the heavy trucks they have." Paco suggested.

"Good idea!" the priest   replied.

They jumped in the jeep and were off in seconds.

Not more than several minutes later. The lead Hummer passed the spot they had just left and drove on to the dirt road a few hundred yards beyond that would take the caravan of trucks through the village creating an uproar of commotion.

By the time they reached the abandoned shack Paco had driven the old jeep almost half-way to the church.

At the church Myles took Paco aside and swore him to secrecy, Paco took it well as it hurt him to think he would betray the man and the faith he loved more than life.

The priest came into the small windowless room underneath the rectory and behind a life-sized statue of Saint Francis of Assisi.

"Thank you father". Alex said kissing his hand, followed by Illapa.

"Don't thank me just yet mate, we are not out of the woods. I think they will take today and tomorrow and search the jungle for you, but ultimately they will come back here and I will have to face them and their questions, I will pray for guidance and deliverance. I suggest you both do the same. I promise you everything will be fine if we trust in the Lord."

He hugged them both.

"Mum's the word, no noise and no going outside without me. Either Paco or Dominique or I will bring you food once a day. You will split it into meals. We cannot risk exposure or involve anyone else. God Bless You!"

"God Bless you father."

Later That Day.

"Para! Stop it we are in a church and you can't keep your hands off me...bestia!(beast!)" she whispered playfully.

"But I want you so bad right now!" He whispered back nibbling on her ears.

"Alex...I am too scared to fight you!" She turned as she softly resisted.

They made love quietly. It would be different without the usual sounds of passion but the excitement of the forbidden pleasure only enhanced their lovemaking. He kept his mouth over hers to muffle her sounds. Afterwards they lay in each others arms longer than usual. And Alex offered a new prayer that made her smile.

"Thank you Lord for this gift of love you have given us. We offer you our bodies and souls we are yours forever."

"I will not leave your side; if we are caught I would rather die than be separated from you."

"I was thinking the same thing. I don't want to live without you."

"Then we must get a gun, you will shoot me and then yourself." She could still procure that young girl in he hills of Peru.

"No, we will throw ourselves off the sacrificial perch in Yaguas."

"I will hold your hand   when we jump together; I want to go to the Lord with you."

"Let's pray for a miracle." Alex added.

The Next Morning.

"Why do you love me?" she said to him.

"Because you are part of me, and I cannot separate you from my soul. You are me and I am you. God made us one flesh."

She turned to him and kissed him.

"Do you want some coffee? He offered.

"I want a baby, Alex, I want your baby."

"Illa, you want to tell the whole world? Please keep your voice down".

"Mi amor I didn't mean to speak so loud, please forgive me, why don't you have some coffee".

Alex began to pace the dirt floor.

"I don't want any damn coffee; I want to get out of here!"

"Oh God, look who's yelling now?"

"So what!" Alex folded himself into the nearest chair.

"I'm going to take a look outside."

"What! I'm going with you."

"Ok, but be quiet and don't talk."

They sneaked out of their cell and made their way out into the church office quietly.

From the office they made their way to the small window that overlooked the town square.

They both looked through the window at the soldiers outside and the townspeople strolling by on their way. It was just an instant, but Alex felt a chill and he let out a sigh, which made Illapa look at him. And then she saw her.

The intricacies of the female mind were as foreign to Alex as the clouds in the sky. After a few moments of puzzlement, he turned to Illapa and told her they must get back to their room. She could see that he was deep in thought.

"What's wrong, mi amor?"

"I'ts all right, we need to talk to the priest." Lets go.

A Few Minutes Later.

"Oh, Jesus," Alex let the words escape from his lips as he paced the floor.

Illapa brought him a cup with coffee and he took it with an air of one doomed, going to meet his fate. Alex overdramatized situations, but then, she was beginning to know him as the kind of man who did not respond to subtle hints, and some things had to be dragged right before his nose before he would get to the point.

"Illa, please let me think," it was a father admonishing the child.

She let him alone for the moment, something she had never done before.

Alex knelt and began to   pray. She knelt by his side and prayed with him.

When he finished he turned to her and kissed her on the lips tenderly.

"Mi amor, the woman outside with the troops is my wife Linda." He let the words sink slowly, and held her close to him.

"What!!!?" She half-screamed pushing him away.

"Why is she here? She's still in love with you, I bet a million dollars! I'll slice her throat, I'll…"

"Baby calm down I don't know why she is here. I need to talk to Father so that I can find out."

"What kind of a fool are you? Of course she's in love with you, why else would she be here? Don't touch me!" Alex moved away from her.

"I wish I could talk to Mark, he knows for sure."

"And who is Mark?"

"Her father, I told you about the man who always helped me."

"And why is he not here?"

"You need to calm down and I need to talk to Father."

She moved away from him and sank down on their bed, looking at him with eyes that reproached him. He stayed on his side of the room.

The Next Day.

The Priest brought them their food early the next day. As

soon as he was in the room   Alex asked him to sit down.

"Father we must talk to you. We went outside yesterday."

"What! I told you to stay in here; you could put the whole village in danger."

"Father, forgive us, but please, the blond American woman we saw outside with the troops, who is she?"

"She is in charge, the leader of the Americans and the Colombian Captain seems to be under her command also."

"What is her name?" Alex asked the priest.

"Special Agent Linda Russo" I believe is the name she gave me.

"I think she is with the CIA" That is what the people are saying.

"Father...she is my wife"

The words came with a pleading. Alex looked at Father Crewes, he looked back at him but the face was not the one of a priest, but a man, a man who loved and lost.

"Oh Lord," was all he said.

A Few Minutes Later.

Fr. Crewes knelt at the altar of his church and prayed for wisdom and guidance.

The Jesus on the cross in his church was a remarkable work of art. Jesus was not lying on the cross; he was blending into the Cross as if they were one. What a wonderful way to see the Savior, Myles thought, in perfect unison with his destiny.

The man who carved it   was a local artisan with no education or training who had been carving wood all his life. When he met the new father he was moved by his words of hope. He had come to eat at the church many times when he had no money or food. He was never turned away without a meal or some coins.

He found the piece of mahogany almost cut to the perfect dimensions by a bolt of lightning one day as he walked through the forest. He stood and looked at it for a long time until he saw the Christ in the Cross. He brought his horse and tied him to the heavy wood and dragged it to his carving shed. He walked alongside his horse urging him on and fell several times along the way, like Jesus did on the Via Dolorosa. When he finally reached his home, he found that he was not tired at all. He picked up his tools and began to carve the wood immediately.

When he took the statue to the church the whole town came to look and marvel at his work. They made a special collection for him and he was able buy more materials and then a distributor that sold his artworks in Bogota, he would never go hungry again. Instead he gave generously to his church and taught carving to all those who came by his shed.

Fr. Myles had the Christ hung from thin wires from the ceiling, and it hung just above the altar and not on the wall. His Christ appeared to be on his way to heaven pointing the way to Salvation for all who gazed upon him.

And now Fr. Myles knelt just below the Savior and prayed that this fiasco would end in Peace. That those in most need of the Lord's presence would   have the wisdom to accept his will.

The Next Day.

Linda had set up her headquarters in a rooming house about a quarter-mile from the church. She was busy writing an email to the home office when Fr. Crewes came in to her makeshift office unannounced.

She saved her email for later and faced him.

"How are you today father?"

"A bit worried, I'm afraid."

"I think I know why." She looked at him with the unsympathetic look of a person in power.

"I have a favor to ask of you."

"I don't think you are in any position to ask for favors, you are harboring two fugitives, two murderers under the sanctuary of your church. I need for you to turn them over to me at once."

"Of course I will do what is right, but first I ask that you meet with me and them alone, without your men."

"I don't see why I should."

"Please do me this favor. They will not resist arrest nor fight you. I guarantee this."

Linda looked at the priest. She had received the tip from an informant just an hour ago and was about to inform the home office when the priest interrupted her. She was figuring out how to proceed with the extraction when he made his tempting offer.

"All right, let's go." She began to strap-on her gun.

"That will not be necessary I assure you."

It was his eyes, Linda figured, that moved her and gave her a sense of peace and well-being.

"Very well."

The priest led the way. They walked slowly along the road toward the church leaving the town behind. As she walked Linda put her hand in her pockets and played with her key chain. She could hear the keys clinking. She began to have lustful thoughts and closed her eyes for a second thinking of embracing her husband. But then she shook her head and her mind cleared and she knew what lay ahead was not an embrace it was a confrontation. No matter what happened she was very close to bringing closure to her life.

She was suddenly very hot after just walking a couple of blocks. She took out a handkerchief and began to swipe her neck and face.

A couple of boys ran up to them and began walking with them, each one holding on to the hand of the priest. He was gentle with them but firm when he told them to go to their house. They did as he said.

"You have a way with the people." She said to him.

"You have to know life to be a good priest." His voice came soothing with reverence. She looked at him again for she needed to see his eyes one more time before she went into the

Church.

Alex could not look Illapa in the face. She knew he was nervous and worried. But she also knew she could not help him with this. It would be the same as if she had met her father while he was alive. How would she have acted? Would she have embraced him with tears and forgiveness or would she have beat the shit out of him and shot him in the head? She felt Alex's pain. But thankfully she had found the Grace of God and she prayed that it would guide Alex and the woman that had their future in her hands.

A soft knock on the door made them both look at each other. Illapa ran into his arms.

"I Love You, no matter what happens."

Alex gently kissed her forehead and sat her on the bed. He went to the door and opened it.

Fr. Myles came in through the door and whispered something in his ear and embraced him. He then went to Illapa and embraced her. Alex walked out the door and closed it behind him.

When he saw her standing in the corner of the little rectory office the air suddenly became thick, the energy left his body.

She saw him then, so she walked slowly towards him until she could see his eyes. Then he lifted his arm which seemed to weigh a ton and reached for her softly. As his hand reached out towards her face, she was no longer angry. His eyes were the same as the priest's. She was a woman again, the same woman with the fervent desire to be   loved by a man. His hand reached her cheek and the spark created by his touch moved her like a sea storm and swept her body out to sea.

For a moment in time everything was new. The two of them were thrust into this confused state and embraced.

They clung to each other for a long time not wanting to talk or say anything that would bring them back to the moment.

She broke free and retreated to her corner, wiping her face and eyes.

"I have a job to do!" She said trying to subdue her tears.

"So have I." He said kneeling down.

"Linda, can you forgive me for leaving you, for hurting you, for not being there for you. I was wrong, so very wrong and sinful, how can I ever make it up to you?"

"You can't, you're going to prison for the rest of your life!"

"If that will make it right for you I'm ready to face my penance."

All I ask is that you spare Illapa. She deserves a second chance. Let her stay here and serve the Lord with the priest and her people. If you grant me this wish I will cooperate and do everything you ask of me.

"I'm sorry I have already promised the local agencies that they can arrest her. She has quite a record. If she's lucky they will shoot her right here and not turn her over to the Peruvian government." She spoke softly but sternly, even though she was lying. She had not sent in her report.

"It's me you want   Linda, please let her go, I beg you. The woman in there is not the woman in your files."

"NO" was all she said.

Fr. Myles came into the room and went to Linda and gently took her arm and walked her to a quiet bench overlooking the life-sized statue of Our Lady of Guadalupe. The statue was old, the gold inlay was missing, and the wood and paint worn and cracked. But she looked out at anyone who gazed at her as if they were the only ones in the room. It was a peaceful glance.

Linda looked at the Virgins face and tried to look away. But she looked back and she felt uncomfortable, but safe. She did not want to stay but something held her back.

Alex moved away towards Illapa who had come out into the church and guided her back to their room. Father Myles closed the door behind them.

Fr. Myles began with a prayer.

"Blessed Mother hear our prayer, be our advocate with your beloved Son, our Savior, pray for us Holy Mother of God"

"I know all about you and Alex."

Linda looked at the priest with pain in her eyes, but her eyes did not move Myles. He had seen those eyes before.

"You know nothing about me."

"I know everything there is to know about loss and suffering."

"Then you can understand why I have to take them back to face Justice." She tried to sound forceful but the priest was unmoved.

"Whose justice? Yours or God's?"

"Humanity's". She said

"I see, so you are doing it for you fellow man, imprison two criminals to protect society, is that it".

"Yes." She said, not convinced.

"Then you have no personal vendetta or agenda, you are acting on behalf of your office and humanity?"

The same "Yes."

"If I can convince you that the two souls in that room are not who you think they are will you consider granting them a second chance?"

"I...have a duty". She said.

"I agree, you have a duty to perform for humanity."

"Yes." She said.

"Well then, let me tell you about humanity and Love."

Fr. Myles began to tell her about his life, it was the first time he told anyone his testimony since he had arrived in the mountains. Then he told her about Alex and Illapa, about Paco, the Jesus in the Church. And finally about forgiveness and Fr. Louis.

Towards the end she began to cry. At first softly with barely a trickle of a tear coming down from the sea blue eyes. Then she bowed her head and let them come. All at once. She could not stop. He reached for her with his arms and slowly brought her to him and she nestled in his embrace and cried until she was ready to speak.

"Oh father, I have this terrible pain inside me. It is unbearable; I don't know how to stop it." She spoke softly still resting her head on his chest.

"My child, you must let this pain out, cast it aside, I can help you, tell me about your pain?"

"Father I have sinned against humanity, the most horrible of sins, I've never told anyone…I killed my unborn child."

She cried again, the tears and sobs in anguish accompanied a plea.

"Oh God, help me, forgive me. Frank forgive me for lying to you."

"Go on my child."

"Father I want to tell you everything. I need to tell you everything." She was eager now, there was no need for holding back nor for thinking, this was her chance to come clean, to lay it all on the line, place it at the foot of the Cross. She told him everything.

When Linda was finished she felt like a new woman. There was a peace in her whole being that she had never known before. She looked at the priest with a new face.

"Linda you have carried your sins inside you long-enough. God has opened your heart and will give you a second chance. You know what to do. You must pray each day for the rest of your life for the soul of your unborn child. You must seek out your friend Frank and ask for his forgiveness. You must do something to help the children of this world."

"Father, I feel as if I've been let off too easy, I feel as if I need more punishment."

"Why do you feel this? Do you think you are beyond the forgiveness of sins by our Savior?"

"No, what I mean is that I don't understand, but I want to. Is it really this easy to be forgiven…to forgive?"

"I think that you have learned that life is not easy. But you have God to help you, if you let him. The hardest part for you will be to let him. This is a choice that you must make. He gave us *"Free Will"* we must decide where we want to go in our lives. I hope you decide to come to the Lord."

"Yes, father I want to feel like this for the rest of my life."

"Then find a Church back home and devote your life to Him. It will not be easy, nothing worthwhile ever is. Find a good Spiritual Advisor. I suggest you find one that is accessible and close by. But you can call or write me, I will always be there for you."

Linda stood up finally and walked over to the statue. She looked into her eyes for several minutes and prayed.

When she was finished she turned and faced the priest.

"What would God want me to do about them?"

"Why don't we pray together and ask for his guidance."

They both knelt by the altar and prayed, later she left him alone in the Church.

It was late afternoon as Linda walked hurriedly back to her makeshift office. She looked across the fertile valley to the west as the sun was low on the sky hanging like an incandescent ball; it was going down in between the mountains. The green of the valley framed the picture   and she stopped to look. Everything looked new. Palms swayed with the breeze and when it reached her face she smiled.

Before she could reach her office two of her officers came running towards her.

"Linda, they are running again towards the lowlands, I think they are going to try for the Amazon."

"Go and get the Humvee's and pick me up here as fast as you can. And get Capt. Alvarez and his men to follow us." For a second she was the old Linda again. She must hold it together for it to work.

Once the convoy of her men and Capt. Alvarez's had gathered in the street, she came and got in the lead car with Paco trailing behind her.

"Ok let's go up the south road, this is my informant and he knows where they are going."

The convoy sped by the Church and down the road, raising dust and rustling the leaves of the banana trees huddled in their groupings. The powerful and resilient thick leaves arching in splendor waved good-bye in unison.

The road cut through the planted fields of corn on either side. After the corn came a plain sloping downwards away from the mountains. But they took a small road that headed straight for the sun and the mountains.

They came rushing out of the valley and headed up the steep grade and up the mountain. The forest engulfed them and they were surrounded by trees with limbs and branches that brushed the sides of the vehicles making a scraping noise as it made its way up the narrow road.

"How much further?" Linda asked Paco.

"Just about another three miles. You must tell them to slow down we will have to walk to the place."

"What place?" She said.

"The Altar".

"What Altar?"

"The Ancient Altar where the ancient ones sacrificed the virgins."

"What are you talking about?" The driver shot back.

"Listen to me Paco, why are they coming here?" Linda asked him.

"They are going to jump." He said and bowed his head.

"You've got to be kidding me!" said the driver.

"Paco, how do you know this?" Linda asked.

"He told me."

"Who told you?"

"The man, the husband, he said they were not going to prison, they would die before spending the rest of their lives in prison."

"And the girl, did she go along with this?"

"Yes, she said she would never leave him."

"That's just great, just when we had them." The driver said.

"How much further?" Linda asked him again.

"Stop ahead at that clearing, (he pointed) we go on foot

the rest of the way."

They ran in the direction that Paco pointed, and left him behind.

After a few minutes they came to a clearing just barely visible through the heavy brush. Off to one side was a jeep and an old truck with the passenger door wide open.

Paco caught up with them and made for a small opening through the trees. Linda and her men were close behind. They heard Capt. Alvarez arrive but did not wait for them.

Paco led them up a rocky path. Before they got to their destination they could hear a woman crying.

They hurried.

When at last the path opened in front of them they could see Paco's wife Dominique and Fr. Crewes kneeling. The priest was praying. Dominique was crying.

Paco went to his wife and she ran into his arms.

"Que paso mi vida?" (What happened my Love?) He said to her.

Linda and the rest awaited her reply.

"Se tiraron!". (They jumped)

Linda and her men walked up to the edge.

As they looked at the precipice beneath them they could not imagine anyone surviving the fall.

Almost two hundred feet below was a grotto, the small lagoon was pitch black in color surrounded by rock on all sides except for one small opening where water rushed through a space about 12 feet wide and cascaded down in a waterfall that poured tons of water into the   river where it flowed through white water rapids into a canyon below.

"Father, what can you tell me?" She knelt down next to the priest.

"When we got here there was no one here."

"Do you think they jumped and their bodies are still in the grotto?" She asked.

He crossed himself and bowed his head. "Suicide is a sin."

Dominique stopped her crying and spoke to Linda.

"I saw the bodies go over the falls and into the river. If they are not torn to shreds by the rapids they will end up in the basin. Where I'm afraid the animals and crocodiles will most likely..." she could not end the sentence but buried her head once more into Paco's chest.

"Linda knelt down and began to cry softly. Her second came over and put his arms around her and held her until her tears subsided.

Epilogue

Chinese Proverb taught to children: "Siaosin" (Make thy heart small)

Disney World, Orlando, Florida Present Day

Linda did not need an alarm to wake up. She was awakened by a gentle tug and the whisper of a sweet voice.

"Mommy, wake up its time to wake up and go". Chloe, her daughter was kneeling by the bed with her head on her hands and her elbows firmly planted on the bed.

"Can't we sleep a little more; your father and I are very tired."

"No, you promised today we go on the White Water ride, you promised."

"OK, Ok but let your   father sleep some more."

"Who can sleep with all this racket, who's making all this noise, a mouse?"

Her husband rolled over and kissed Linda's shoulder.

"Daddy, let's all get up and go on the White Water ride." Chloe said as she climbed over her mother and into the arms of her father who tickled her on her ribs and made her squeal.

"Honey, you're too small to go on that ride, you are going to be terrified." He admonished.

From the door of the bedroom appeared a young boy holding a teddy bear with no eyes and almost no fur.

"Are we going now?" he said and jumped in the bed with his sister.

"Come on Myles, the more the merrier." Linda said acknowledging defeat.

It was the middle of the Florida Winter. Cool evenings and mornings with very comfortable days. But up in central Florida in Orlando where they were now it was colder than Miami. Linda liked the cool weather and looked forward to it.

Her figure was not perfectly thin anymore. A precocious eight-year old daughter and boy of six along with a new career as a housewife and pro-bono children's advocate for the ACLU had taken their toll. She was still a head-turner. And her husband Frank reminded her often.

"You are beautiful." He said to her last night after the kids were asleep and he made love to her quietly under the sheets.

The Hotel was not the best in Orlando but it was the

closest to Disney World that   they could afford this time of the year. Frank was not the successful Stockbroker that he once was. He had learned the hard way that life was not about success and wealth. Linda had saved him from himself. When she showed up one day at his office and asked if they could talk.

All the hurt and pain was washed from his memory that afternoon when they walked and talked and she asked him to forgive her. Then she told him her story. And when she was finished, he told her that none of it mattered. He loved her. He never stopped loving her. From that moment his life changed for the better. He came back to the church at her urging, was confirmed in the Catholic faith and asked her to marry him on the day of his confirmation during Easter. She said yes, with one condition. If they had a son they would name him Myles.

This cool morning as they drove to Disney World Linda thanked God silently as they passed a church. It was an old building with a tall steeple that stood out among the modern motels and restaurants that gave Orlando that touristy feel.

"Your mustache looks great now that it's filled-in." Linda said. "It looks just like Tom Selleck's." She teased.

Frank was still a handsome man of almost fifty with salt-pepper hair growing more natural than when was younger, he liked it this way now to match a freer spirit.

"Well he is a fine looking man, I'm glad you didn't say Groucho Marx."

"Who's "Grouch Marks?" Asked Chloe.

"A very funny man who's now in Heaven."

"Was he as funny as Robin Williams?" her curiosity peaked.

"As a matter of fact, he was just as zany and funny. Don't you think honey?" she said to her husband.

"I kind of like Robin, but yes I can see the same wackiness."

"Will you show me a movie of Groucho someday?" Chloe asked.

"Absolutely baby as soon as we get back home."

The park was full of visitors, as usual. Throngs of people rushed past them as they walked the streets and visited all their favorite attractions and rides.

In the afternoon when Myles began to complain that he was tired. They sat and ate some ice cream and rested.

"Mom, I'm going to drink some water." Chloe said as she walked to the fountain a few feet away from their table.

When she got to the fountain it was too high for her to reach the water. Her mother noticed this and pushed Myles's stroller to the side to get up and to go to her daughter. She looked away for just an instant. When she got up to go to Chloe, she was startled to see a man lift her up so that she could reach the water. Normally Chloe would resist, but she was too busy looking at the attractive dark skinned boy with long dark straight hair that stood near her awaiting his turn and who was smiling at her.

Linda walked towards them without dread, it was strange. A mother's first instinct is to protect her children. She did not have any of these   dreadful feelings as she came up to them.

"Thanks so much, I was coming to…"

She stared into the face of Alex.

"Oh sweet Jesus." He said breathlessly.

They looked at each other in awesome wonder for an instant.

"Linda, Wow… how are you?"

"I'm good." She smiled at him.

There was an awkward moment followed by a strange composed look of marvel. They slowly embraced for a tongue-tied moment.

"And you…is this your son?"

"I'm Mark," said the boy holding out his hand to her.

"Mommy you know them?" Chloe said excitedly.

"Yes, dear." And after a pause added "they're old friends of your grandfather."

"You have the same name as my grandpa, I call him Papo. I'm Chloe." And she reached out for the boys hand and shook it.

Illapa approached them pushing a stroller with a beautiful girl asleep in its folds. The Princess' hair was shorter, shoulder-length with some grey streaking the raven-black hair that she had tied with one single bungee. She was visibly pregnant.

"Well, I guess some introductions are in order." Alex said looking around and shaking Frank's hand.

"I'm Vincent", he looked at Linda for endorsement, "and this is my wife, Guadalupe."

"Everyone calls her Lupe." their son added.

"And in the stroller is Michelle, taking a nap, as usual."

"I'm Frank and I'm very pleased to meet you at last, they both smiled, "and this precocious little girl…"

"Dad, I'm not a little girl." Chloe protested trying to impress the boy.

"Ok, my big girl Chloe, and in our stroller here also taking a nap is our son Myles."

"This is a wonderful coincidence. What are the chances that we would meet here of all places with so many people?" Linda said.

"I don't think it's a coincidence." Lupe added.

Lupe and Linda exchanged a knowing glance.

"We were going to the White Water Ride, why don't you join us?" said Frank.

"Yea, Pop, can we go with them." young Mark said.

"Sure, OK sweetheart?" Vincent looked at Lupe.

"OK, but you aren't getting me on that ride." She said firmly.

"I'll hold your hand." Chloe said taking Lupe's hand.

"You are very pretty." Chloe added.

"Thank you, Chloe, so are you." They smiled.

Frank walked in front pushing the stroller and Mark walked beside him.

"How old are you Mark?" said Frank

"Im nine, almost ten." He answered

Lupe followed still holding hands with Chloe.

"I'm a little afraid of the rapids too." Chloe said to the princess.

"Well, if we stick together they can't make us go; I'll tell them I need you to help me looking after Michelle. How's that?

"OK."

Vincent and Linda walked behind them.

"What a lovely sight." Linda said to him.

Vincent looked at her, she looked back. Then he said.

"We are truly blessed."

Acknowledgments

My gratitude goes out to the many wonderful people who helped and guided me on this book. First and foremost I thank God and his infinite mercy for giving me the gift of Grace to write my stories.

And speaking of Grace I would like to thank my beautiful wife Grace for liking this story and taking me to Machu Picchu to make it better and being there for me with love, affection and support, she is the rock we all lean on.

To my three wonderful children, Ariana for her editing and advice, to Vince for inspiring me, and to Frank who designed the beautiful cover and offered some good editing/formatting as well, this book is dedicated to them.

To my son and daughters in law, Diri, Mari and Cesar. Many thanks for putting up with the Fernandez clan.

To my lovely and adorable granddaughters, Monica, Isabella, Chloe, Sabrina, Ella Mia, and Maya you make me want to be the best I can be.

A special thanks to Peggy Olin Fucci the mother of my oldest granddaughter Monica. She is my inspiration for Illapa. A Peruvian beauty with a rich family history.

To those who are no longer with us, to their memory and with my gratitude for the stories they provided and the rich wonderful lives they shared with me. My father and mother, Angelito and Rita, to my sister Marina, my uncle Victor (Tiotovi), my cousin and mentor Jack Denson, my father and mother in law, Leo and Grace and our grandparents whose lives inspired me and my characters.

To my editor, Star Bradley and her daughter Zoe. Star has taken over for my beloved sister Marina and like her mother did a fantastic job. At times she reminded me of her artistic and talented mother but mostly she was a tough critic who, like all good editors, was right most of the time.

To Orlando Rodriguez and David Goldberg my friends, who read my manuscript and offered good advice and editing, I could wish for no better readers or friends.

To my brother Joe, who always reads my work and offers some insight that amazes me.

In memory of my great and irreplaceable friends Valentin Gonzalez and Alberto Menacho voracious readers who made me laugh and brought great comfort in this troubled world, they both read the early manuscript and offered invaluable feedback that I took to heart and made this a better story.

To my friend Robert Ladner, a local Pastor, for his reading the final manuscript and checking its theological context and giving me a heartfelt endorsement.

To my friends and neighbors at Silver Shores and the Free Press in Key Largo where the bulk of this story was written, I will never forget those wonderful years living and writing in paradise.

And finally to these special friends and fans who make me want to write more stories for them to enjoy. Many of their names appear in the book as my way to honor them: my aunt Marta Fernandez and my cousins, Luis and Victor Fernandez, Vivian and Jose Suarez, Raul De Quesada, Al Soler, Jack Denson, Jr., Donna Proffitt Denson, Gene Denson, Archibaldo Vasquez, Tanya Duarte, Pedro and Jaime Valdivia, Johnny McManus and Dee Millares, Edgar and Marta Fernandez,

Henry Valls, Rodolfo "Rudy" Rodriguez, Alejandro and Christy Crespo, Iñaki Saizarbitoria, Manny & Maria Vasquez, Lester Kates, Rene Larriu, Johnny Hugo, Emilio Lopez, Al Rivera, Jr., Mary Camejo, Paco Panceira, Michelle Beltran, Maria Elena Garcia, Luis Boue, Willy Castro, Rock and Heather Salt, Martin Pinilla, Agustin Barreiro, Jose Luis Salgado , Raul Echarte, Bill Edmonds, Frank Bickford, John Sagarribay and fellow author Owen Parr. And to all my Emmaus and Kairos sisters and brothers.

Simon Vincent

About the Author

Simon Vincent is the pen name of Angel Vicente Fernandez, Jr. who was born in Cuba in 1951.

He is the author of **"Waypoint 90-In the Chambers of The Sea"** his first novel published in 2003. **"Sea Lust",** a collection of poetry published in 2007 exploring the deeply felt emotions of a heart that is searching, seeking its own unique way through the labyrinth of human emotions and experiences that make up a life. He edited and published, **"Memorias De Un Taquigrafo"**, his late father's memoirs, in 1993.

Following his family's exile from Cuba in 1960, Angel lived in Miami, New York City, Austin, Texas, and Key Largo, Florida.

Angel attended the University of Texas at Austin earning a B.A. in Government in 1973. For over twenty five years he was devoted to a career in International Banking and Finance.

Currently, he lives in Miami where he fishes, plays Golf and writes, not always in that order.

You can email him at: Simon@simonvincent.com and visit his Blog at: http://simonvincent-author.blogspot.com/

www.simonvincent.com